"My sister isn't stu[...]
And I'm going to p[...]

"How are you going to do that?" Ainsley asked. "I can't imagine they'll just let you poke around the retreat and ask accusatory questions."

"They won't," he agreed. "Which is why I'm going there undercover."

Ainsley frowned. "What do you mean?" There was a note of concern in her tone, and for a second, he wondered if she was worried about him getting into trouble.

"I'm going to pretend to be a client, there with my wife. We're both going to offer them a bribe, then find out which person they decide to help."

"Oh." Ainsley visibly relaxed, apparently assuming she'd deduced his request. "So do you need me to draw up some sham paperwork that your fake wife wants you to nullify?"

"Nope." Santiago shook his head, nerves tingling in his belly as he arrived at his real reason for coming to Ainsley's office. "I want you to be my wife."

* * *

Book eight of The Coltons of Mustang Valley

* * *

**If you're on Twitter, tell us what you
think of Harlequin Romantic Suspense!
#harlequinromsuspense**

Dear Reader,

Welcome back to the world of the Coltons! This is one family that is never boring, and I always love writing about these men and women and their exploits.

Ainsley and Santiago have a shared history that is bittersweet. But when the chips are down, they know they can turn to each other for help. And that's exactly what they do. The only question is, can they overcome the issues from their past to focus on the problems of the present?

I hope you enjoy reading their story as much as I enjoyed writing it! Happy reading!

Lara

COLTON'S UNDERCOVER REUNION

Lara Lacombe

HARLEQUIN
ROMANTIC
SUSPENSE

Special thanks and acknowledgment are given to
Lara Lacombe for her contribution to
The Coltons of Mustang Valley miniseries.

Recycling programs
for this product may
not exist in your area.

ISBN-13: 978-1-335-62652-3

Colton's Undercover Reunion

Copyright © 2020 by Harlequin Books S.A.

This edition published by arrangement with Harlequin Books S.A.

For questions and comments about the quality of this book, please contact us at CustomerService@Harlequin.com.

Harlequin Enterprises ULC
22 Adelaide St. West, 40th Floor
Toronto, Ontario M5H 4E3, Canada
www.Harlequin.com

Printed in U.S.A.

Lara Lacombe earned a PhD in microbiology and immunology and worked in several labs across the country before moving into the classroom. Her day job as a college science professor gives her time to pursue her other love—writing fast-paced romantic suspense with smart, nerdy heroines and dangerously attractive heroes. She loves to hear from readers! Find her on the web or contact her at laralacombewriter@gmail.com.

Books by Lara Lacombe

Harlequin
Romantic Suspense

The Coltons of Mustang Valley

Colton's Undercover Reunion

Rangers of Big Bend

Ranger's Justice
Ranger's Baby Rescue
The Ranger's Reunion Threat

The Coltons of Roaring Springs

Colton's Covert Baby

The Coltons of Red Ridge

Colton K-9 Bodyguard

Doctors in Danger

Enticed by the Operative
Dr. Do-or-Die
Her Lieutenant Protector

The Coltons of Shadow Creek

Pregnant by the Colton Cowboy

The Coltons of Texas

Colton Baby Homecoming

Deadly Contact
Fatal Fallout
Lethal Lies
Killer Exposure
Killer Season

Visit the Author Profile page at Harlequin.com for more titles.

This one is for my mom,
who helps make it all possible.

Chapter 1

Ainsley Colton closed her eyes and let the soothing sounds of ocean waves wash over her.

Deep breath in. Exhale.

Again.

Her muscles relaxed as she repeated the breathing exercises, and gradually, she felt the knots in her stomach ease.

She wasn't normally one for meditation. But with all the stress in her life, she was willing to try anything if it meant staving off a stomach ulcer, or worse.

"You've got to find some way to unplug," Dr. Bleaker had said. She'd looked up at Ainsley during her last visit, dark brown eyes serious behind her gold wire-rimmed glasses. "I mean it, Ainsley. These headaches, your stomach pain—all the tests show there's nothing wrong with you physically. Which means these issues are due to stress. Are you getting enough sleep? Are you exercising at all?"

Ainsley had bit her tongue to keep from laughing at the doctor. She knew the older woman meant well, but seriously? Her father had been shot and her brother Ace was the prime suspect, thanks to an anonymous email someone had sent to the board of her family's company, Colton Oil, that said Ace wasn't a biological Colton. Normally, something like that wouldn't matter, but there was a small clause in the bylaws of the corporation that stated the CEO of the company had to be a Colton by blood. Her father, never one for subtleties, didn't hesitate to oust Ace when the DNA test confirmed that Ace was in fact not a Colton. Her father had been shot soon after his decision, and there were a lot of fingers pointing at her brother.

As the corporate attorney for Colton Oil, she was right in the middle of the legal issues surrounding the company's change in leadership. And as a sister and daughter, her heart had been bruised and battered by the events of the past few months. Ace might not be her brother by blood, but she'd grown up with him. He'd always be her family. It pained her to think of how he must be feeling right now, especially after the things their father had said and done to him. And Ace couldn't have shot Payne. As for the old man, she loved him, too. He wasn't perfect, but he was her dad. Payne Colton was such a force of nature, she couldn't imagine the world without him in it. If only he'd wake up from his coma!

"I mean it, Ainsley," the doctor had said, interrupting her thoughts. "I know you're busy. But if you don't make time for your health, you're going to wind up with an ulcer or a heart attack. Don't work yourself to death. You're only thirty-seven. Your best years are still ahead of you."

Ainsley had smiled and thanked the woman, then hurried back to her office to deal with the latest crisis. But as she'd washed down her fifth antacid of the day with a gulp of stale coffee, she'd been forced to admit Dr. Bleaker was right. She did need to find a way to relax.

So she'd done a little research and decided meditation might be a good option. She didn't have time for yoga classes or a gym membership. But she could carve out fifteen minutes a day to listen to ocean sounds and breathe deeply.

Her cell phone vibrated on her desk, a soft buzz she registered over the meditation soundtrack. She cracked one eye open and stared at it, considering. Should she—?

No, she decided firmly. This meditation stuff wasn't going to help her unless she actually took it seriously. That meant no interruptions. It was only fifteen minutes of her day—the world could wait.

The buzzing stopped. Almost immediately, she

heard the muted ring of her secretary's office phone. Someone really wanted to talk to her. Oh, well. Candace would take a message.

Deep breath in—

The door opened, making her jump. "Ms. Colton?" Candace sounded deeply apologetic. "I know you don't want to be disturbed right now, but your brother is on the line and he says it's an emergency."

"Which brother?" Ainsley kept her eyes closed, tried to stay focused on her breathing. *I'm on a beach*, she told herself. If only that were true!

"It's Asa," Candace replied, using Ace's birth name rather than the nickname his friends and family had adopted.

Ainsley's eyes snapped open, all thoughts of relaxation disappearing between one heartbeat and the next. "I'll take the call," she said, forcing her voice to remain calm. She got to her feet and nodded at Candace, fighting the urge to lunge for the phone that sat on her desk a few feet away. "Thank you."

Candace nodded and backed out of the room, closing the door quietly behind her. Ainsley swore softly as she stepped over to her desk and picked up the receiver.

"Ace?"

"Ainsley, thank God! Why aren't you answering your cell?" He sounded flustered. Ainsley felt her muscles tense all over again. *So much for meditation*, she thought wryly.

"Never mind that. What's going on? You told Candace it was an emergency."

"It is! The police are here. They say they have a warrant."

"Wait, back up." She put her fingers to her forehead and began to massage the spot above her right eyebrow. "Where is here?"

"My condo," Ace said, his tone making it clear this should be obvious. "I came back here after a while. The police are here with a dog and a warrant. What do I do?"

"What are they looking for?" she asked, already walking around the desk to grab her purse from the bottom drawer.

"I don't know yet," he said. "No one's answering my questions."

"Just stay out of the way," she said. "I'm heading there now. I'll be there in a few minutes, and we'll get all this straightened out."

"Hurry," Ace commanded. He was clearly stressed, and she couldn't blame him. She'd be flustered, too, if the police showed up at her door with a K-9 and told her they were going to search the premises.

"I will. Keep your mouth shut," she instructed. "Tell them I'm coming and you'll answer questions once I'm there." With that, she hung up the phone and rushed to the door. "I'll be out for a bit," she said to Candace as she walked past the secretary's desk. "Clear my schedule for the afternoon, please."

"Yes, ma'am," Candace called after her.

Ainsley opted for the stairs, descending as fast as she dared. She was sure the police had their legal ducks in a row—it was highly unlikely they'd risk an illegal search, especially on a member of her family, and given their relation to an MVPD sergeant—but she still wanted to get to Ace quickly. He was already jumpy and freaked out over the events of the past few months, and the last thing she needed was for him to say or do anything that might be interpreted as incriminating.

"Hang on, Ace," she muttered as she climbed behind the wheel of her car. "I'm coming."

It didn't take long to get there. Ainsley opted for the elevator, not wanting to arrive out of breath. As soon as the doors opened, she stepped into the foyer of Ace's condo and glanced around, looking for her brother.

She found him pacing along the far wall of the living room, in front of the stretch of windows that overlooked Mustang Valley. His hair was mussed, and as she watched, he lifted a hand to run through it in a nervous gesture.

He turned on his heel, caught sight of her. Relief flashed across his face, and for an instant, Ainsley felt ten feet tall. It meant a lot to know that her older brother had called her for help, even though technically he wasn't her brother anymore. Regardless, she was going to do everything in her power to prove he hadn't shot their father.

"Hey guys, she's here!" he yelled, alerting the officers to her arrival.

She crossed the room and hugged Ace, feeling the tension in his body as she did. "Did anything happen since we last spoke?"

He shook his head, his brown eyes troubled. "I got out of the way, like you said. They're searching in the bedroom now."

"Did you say something, Ace?" a man's voice called out. Ainsley and Ace both turned to see Spencer Colton walk out of the bedroom. He stopped when he saw Ainsley. "Hey there," he said, offering her a nod.

Ainsley lifted one brow. "Spencer," she replied, greeting her cousin. "Or should I say, Sergeant Colton?" She put a bit of extra emphasis on his last name, and he ducked his head.

"I know it's awkward," he said, walking over to join them. "But I'm here in a professional capacity only."

She and Ace weren't close with their distant cousins, but it was still unorthodox that a family member should be here serving a warrant. She decided to let it slide. If there was an issue, she could always bring it up later.

"May I see the warrant?"

A hurt look flashed across Spencer's face, as though he couldn't believe she would doubt his motives. "Of course," he replied. He pulled a folded packet of papers from his back pocket and passed it to her.

Ainsley began to flip through the papers, scanning to find the information she sought. "A gun?" She looked up at Spencer. "That's what you're hoping to find?"

He nodded, just as Ace interjected, "I don't have a gun!"

Ainsley placed one hand on her brother's arm, silently instructing him to remain quiet. "What's the basis for issuing this warrant?"

Spencer shifted on his feet. "I probably shouldn't tell you this, but…" He shrugged. "Seeing as how you guys are family." He leaned forward and lowered his voice. "We got a tip from someone who said Ace confessed to shooting his father and stashing the gun in his closet."

"That's ludicrous!" Ace said loudly. Ainsley tightened her grip on his arm, her nails digging slightly into his skin. He snapped his mouth shut.

"What's her name?"

Spencer started to shake his head. "Now you know I'm not supposed to—"

Ainsley merely arched her brow and stared him down. Spencer sighed. "All right. Given that Chief Barco approved me working on this case and it could otherwise be a conflict of interest… It was a woman named Destiny Jones."

Beside her, Ainsley felt Ace draw in a breath, preparing to defend himself. She gave his arm a little shake, and he backed down. "Did she say how she knows my client?" She deliberately used formal language, to remind everyone this wasn't a social call.

Spencer glanced at Ace, and twin spots of color appeared high on his cheeks. "She, uh, said it was during an encounter of a personal nature."

"She's lying!" Ace yelled. He shook off Ainsley's hand and stepped forward, bringing him closer to Spencer. "I don't even know a woman named Destiny!"

Spencer held up a hand, palm out to try to diffuse Ace's reaction. "No judgments, man. But we had to check it out."

"So I guess anyone can call you up and spread lies about me, is that it?" Ace threw his arms out in disgust. "This is such a crock of—"

"That seems pretty thin," Ainsley interjected. "How'd you get a judge to sign off on this?" She lifted the warrant, handed it back to Spencer.

"We had enough to get us in the door." His lips pressed together in a thin line. Clearly, her cousin was done talking.

Ace shook his head, still fuming. "Yeah, well, you're not going to find anything," he said. "That woman, whoever she is, is lying."

Seeming sympathy flashed in Spencer's blue eyes. "Between you and me, I hope so. But I still have to do my job."

"Spencer?" A voice called from the bedroom.

"We need you back here. Looks like Boris has found something."

Ace sucked in a breath. Spencer shook his head slightly, then turned. "Coming."

Ainsley waited until her cousin had left the room. Then she grabbed Ace's arm and dragged him over to the foyer, as far away from the bedroom as she could get.

"You need to be straight with me, right now," she said, tugging his shirt for emphasis. "What are they going to find in your bedroom?"

"Nothing!" Ace whispered back urgently. "I swear to you, Ainsley, I didn't shoot Dad. You know I didn't. There is no gun in my room because I didn't do it." He met her eyes unflinchingly, his tone, his expression, everything about him absolutely sincere.

"Then what—"

"I don't know!" he interrupted. She heard the edge of panic in his voice and her heart went out to him. He ran a hand through his hair again, causing the strands to stand on end. "But I can tell you this much—I don't know a Destiny Jones. I haven't been with a woman since—" he cut himself off, the tips of his ears going pink as he looked away. "Well, that doesn't matter. What's important is that whoever this woman is, she's lying."

"Why would a stranger lie about you like that?" Ainsley wondered aloud.

"I don't know," he said. He shook his head. "Maybe it's a business thing? Someone trying to get back at me for something I did earlier? Or for money?"

Ainsley nodded slowly. That was definitely possible. Ace had a reputation as a ruthless businessman, and he had his fair share of professional enemies. Had one of them heard about the recent troubles over at Colton Oil and decided to make things harder on Ace?

She opened her mouth to respond, but before she could say anything, she saw Spencer walk out of the bedroom holding an evidence bag.

"Ace?" he called.

Ainsley and Ace returned to the living room. Her gaze zeroed in on the clear bag in Spencer's hand, and her stomach dropped as she saw its contents.

Spencer lifted his arm, showing Ace the gun. "We're going to need you to come down to the station and answer a few questions."

Three hours later...

Ainsley sank into her desk chair with a sigh, feeling wrung out. She was tired, both from the events of the afternoon and her struggles to manage Ace's reactions to everything.

Her brother had immediately and emphatically insisted the gun that Spencer's scent hound, Boris, had discovered was not his. She believed him, but the police weren't quite as willing to take him at his word. And why should they? A woman had called in a tip saying Ace had a gun in his closet, and lo and behold, they'd found it. It was a compelling piece of evidence, and possibly the weapon that had been used to shoot Payne Colton.

Except, it was all so very neat and tidy. Too neat, in Ainsley's opinion. The more she thought about it, the more plausible Ace's theory about a business or personal rival sounded. It was the perfect way to punish Ace for his steamroller business strategy, and she was willing to bet there were a lot of disgruntled souls he'd left in his wake as CEO of Colton Oil.

But as much as she wanted to help her brother, she was going to have to call in reinforcements. It wouldn't be appropriate for her to handle Ace's legal issues while still working for Colton Oil. Besides, she wasn't a defense attorney, and after the discovery of the gun in Ace's closet, her brother had now become the prime suspect in their father's shooting.

"Don't leave town," Spencer had cautioned after he'd declared Ace was free to go.

"We'll definitely have more questions for you later," Detective Kerry Wilder, their adoptive brother Rafe's fiancée, had added.

"I'm sure you will," Ace had grumbled. "I've always been a suspect."

Ainsley had managed to drag her brother away before his temper had flared again. She understood why he was so upset, but every time he got emotional it only made him appear more guilty.

"Stay here," she'd told him, dropping him off at

his condo. "I know the best defense attorney in the state. I'm going to call in a favor."

"I don't want someone else," Ace had said. "I want you."

"You can't have me," she'd told her brother. "This isn't my specialty. Trust me, this guy is good. You don't need to worry."

"I'm worried as hell," he'd grumbled. "But I do trust you."

She'd been touched by his admission, once again feeling a spurt of pride at the fact that her big brother was relying on her. Now, in the privacy of her office, she allowed herself a little smile.

Her cell phone sat on her desk. She reached out and traced her fingertip along the edge, gathering up her courage to take this next step. She'd promised her brother the best defense attorney in the state. She owed it to him to deliver.

Even if it meant calling the man who'd broken her heart.

She took a deep breath and picked up the phone before she could change her mind. She'd deleted Santiago's number years ago, but it didn't matter. Her fingers danced across the keypad without hesitation, punching in the numbers she still knew by heart.

He picked up on the first ring. "Ainsley." His voice was deep and smooth. A tingle shot down her spine and she closed her eyes, wishing he hadn't answered so quickly. She'd wanted a few more seconds to compose herself, to prepare to speak to him again.

She cleared her throat. "Hello, Santiago. How are you?"

"Better, now that I'm talking to you." He'd always been so charismatic. It seemed the years had done nothing to diminish his charm. "To what do I owe this pleasant surprise?"

Ainsley swallowed hard, pushing down her pride. Ace. She was doing this for her brother. "I need your help."

"Of course," Santiago replied. "Are you in your office?"

She frowned. "Yes. But—"

"Excellent," Santiago said, cutting her off. "I'll be there in five minutes."

"You'll what?" she exclaimed. But he'd already ended the call, leaving her with nothing but a dial tone.

Ainsley hung up and placed the phone on her desk, her thoughts a jumbled mess. He couldn't be coming here. That wasn't the deal. She'd bargained on talking to him only, giving him Ace's information and letting him take things from there. She hadn't intended on seeing him again.

And what was he doing in town anyway? He didn't live in Mustang Valley. It was the only reason she'd been able to get over him after he'd broken her heart years ago. If she'd had to see him all the time, she'd still be pining for the man. His move to New York after their break-up had been a bit of a gift. She'd heard through the professional grapevine he'd returned to Phoenix, but she hadn't expected to find him in the comparatively sleepy town of Mustang Valley.

She lifted her hand, brushing it over her hair. This was really happening. In a few minutes, Santiago Morales was going to walk through her door.

Would her heart be able to handle it?

Damn. She looks good.

Santiago pushed the thought aside and offered a smile to Ainsley's secretary. The woman blushed prettily and nodded before turning to leave. Normally, he'd take such a reaction as a compliment, maybe even an excuse to invite her to dinner. But now that he'd seen Ainsley again, he only had eyes for her.

Had it really been five years since their breakup? Five years since he'd left to chase his dreams in New York City, opting to prioritize his career over his personal life? In some ways, it felt like a lifetime ago. But standing in Ainsley's office, watching the play of emotions on her face as he drew closer, it suddenly seemed like only a few hours had passed since he'd made his choice.

She looked different now. Her brown hair was shorter, falling to her shoulders instead of down her back. God, how he'd loved to wrap those strands around his hands! Her hair had always felt like silk on his skin, a soft caress that had driven him mad.

Even now, just thinking about it gave him goose bumps.

Ainsley watched him approach, her blue eyes guarded and her delicate features arranged in a carefully neutral expression. Her skin was still pale, a testament to the amount of time she spent in her office. She sported some fine lines at the corners of her eyes, and he hoped they were from laughing and not frowning. He'd always wanted the best for her, had always wanted her to be happy.

Which was why he'd left.

He wasn't husband material—never had been, never would be. It was something he'd always known about himself, and given his family history of miserable marriages, he wasn't looking to take on that particular role.

So he'd left, before he could disappoint Ainsley with his shortcomings.

Santiago forced himself to smile as he came to a stop in front of her desk. His arms ached to embrace her, to have her fill the Ainsley-shaped hollow space in his soul that he'd lived with over the past five years. But he could tell by her apprehensive air that such an overture would not be welcomed.

"Ainsley," he said. Just saying her name gave him a kind of relief. After he'd left, he'd done his best to push all thoughts of her to the side. He'd thrown himself into his work, and his efforts had paid off. He'd made a name for himself, first in New York City, then in Phoenix. Coming back to Arizona had never been part of his plan, but when the firm had called a year and a half ago, they'd made him an offer he simply couldn't refuse.

So he'd packed his things and moved back to the land of sun. And Ainsley. He hadn't expected to hear from her—after all, things hadn't ended well between them. Even so, he couldn't deny he'd felt a spark of hope when he'd seen her name on his phone screen. He knew it had taken a lot for her to reach out to him. And while he knew she had zero interest in seeing him again in a personal capacity, part of him wondered if they couldn't find their way to being friends again.

"Hello, Santiago." She didn't offer her hand, so he didn't either. It was clear she didn't want him to touch her, and he always respected a woman's boundaries.

She gestured to the seat behind him. "Please, make yourself comfortable. Would you like something to drink?"

"No, thank you," he replied, lowering himself into the chair. He made an obvious show of studying her face. "You look wonderful," he said simply.

If she appreciated the compliment, she didn't show it. "Thank you," she said flatly. She leaned back a bit in her chair, evidently conducting her own appraisal. "I'm surprised you're in town," she said. "What's a big fish like you doing in such a small pond?"

Ouch. He tried not to wince at the barb. He hadn't used those exact words, but that had been the gist of his argument when he'd left five years ago. "I can't grow my career here," he'd said, gesturing to the window to encompass Mustang Valley. "I'm not going to spend the rest of my life working on drunken assault cases and DUIs." He'd needed to move to New York to take on the kind of high-profile cases that interested him. Given his childhood, he'd known marriage wasn't in his future. He hadn't enjoyed hurting her, but there had been no other way.

"I'm here on family business," he said, running his hand down the length of his tie. But he didn't want to talk about that just yet. First, he wanted to hear her story. "Why don't you tell me how I can help you?"

Ainsley pressed her lips together, and he got the impression that calling him had been a last resort. Worry flared to life in his belly. What was going on? Was she in some kind of trouble? He'd assumed she'd called him on behalf of someone else, but in the face of her obvious reluctance, he had to wonder if he'd been wrong.

"You know I'll help you," he said quietly. He'd never stopped caring for her, probably never would. He'd made it clear when he'd left that he would always be there for her. And even though he'd never expected her to turn to him again, he was pleased that she had now.

She nodded, emotion flashing in her eyes. "It's my brother," she said finally.

Bit by bit, she told him the whole story. The email

to the company's board, the DNA test, her father's shooting. And the gun they'd found today in Ace's condo. He'd heard some of the details before, thanks to news coverage of the story. But she'd filled in several gaps in his knowledge and he realized how convoluted the whole thing actually was.

"He didn't do this," she said, leaning forward a bit. "I know it looks bad right now, but I also know my brother. He's not capable of doing something like this."

Santiago didn't argue. In his experience, people were often very capable of doing shocking things, and often for less motivation that what she'd just outlined. But he wasn't here to argue with Ainsley about the darker aspects of human nature. He'd only met Ace a few times before; he didn't know the man well enough to form an opinion on the matter.

"So are you asking me to advise you?" She wasn't a defense attorney, but he knew she could handle this case if she wanted to, especially with a little help.

She shook her head. "No. I'm asking you to take the case."

He leaned back, considering. What he'd told her earlier was true—he was in town on a family matter. But perhaps he could kill two birds with one stone?

"All right," he said slowly. "I'll take the case."

Relief flashed across Ainsley's face. "Thank you. I'll have a contract drawn up immediately. We will pay your full rate, plus expenses."

Santiago waved this away. "I'm not worried about the money. There's something else I need from you."

Ainsley's eyes filled with wariness, and he felt a wall go up between them. "Oh? What's that?"

"You're not the only one who has a sibling in trouble."

Ainsley arched an eyebrow, silently inviting him to continue.

"It's my sister, Gabriela," he began. "She married a real piece of work. She's been unhappy for a long time, and she agreed to try counseling. They went to this place called The Marriage Institute. It's a few miles outside town—have you heard of it?"

Ainsley shook her head. "No," she said. "Is it like a retreat of some kind?"

"That's exactly what it is," he said, relieved that she seemed to understand. "Gabriela and her husband Eric went, and after a week there, she agreed to sign some paperwork nullifying large sections of their prenuptial agreement, specifically the clauses regarding spousal infidelity and inheritance upon her death."

Ainsley frowned. "That doesn't sound right."

"No, it doesn't," he agreed. "But I looked at the documents and they appear to be solid, from a legal standpoint."

"Why would she sign such a thing? Your parents were always vigilant about your inheritance terms. I'm sure they treated your sister the same way."

Santiago nodded. "Believe me, they did. If anything, they were even more careful with Gabriela's share once she decided to get married." His family's wealth went back generations, thanks to careful stewardship from his great-grandfather and then grandfather. His own parents had added to the layers of protection guarding their money, wanting to ensure their family's future for decades to come. Gabriela's engagement had come with a veritable forest of paperwork for her would-be husband to sign, all in the interest of making sure he couldn't touch a penny of her share of the Morales fortune.

And then his sister had undermined most of it with a stroke of the pen.

"I think Gabriela was coerced into signing the paperwork," he said, leaning forward. "I think this Marriage Institute is a sham, that they don't really care about helping people at all. I think they take bribes from spouses and go to work brainwashing the unsuspecting partner until they agree to see things their spouse's way. That's the only reason Gabriela would sign those papers." He shook his head, frustration rising in his chest the way it always did when he thought about what had happened. "I've spoken to some other people who attended the retreat. They all tell the same story. Gabriela isn't the only one they took advantage of—there are several other people out there who noticed irregularities in their joint accounts that their exes never really explained. Missing funds that were probably used as bribes. My sister isn't stupid. She was tricked. And I'm going to prove it."

"How are you going to do that?" Ainsley asked. "I can't imagine they'll just let you poke around the retreat and ask accusatory questions."

"They won't," he agreed. "Which is why I'm going there undercover."

Ainsley frowned. "What do you mean?" There was a note of concern in her tone, and for a second, he wondered if she was worried about him getting into trouble.

"I'm going to pretend to be a client, there with my wife. We're both going to offer them a bribe, then find out which person they decide to help."

"Oh." Ainsley visibly relaxed, apparently assuming she'd deduced his request. "So do you need me to draw up some sham paperwork that your fake wife wants you to nullify?"

"Nope." Santiago shook his head, nerves tingling in his belly as he arrived at his real reason for coming to Ainsley's office. "I want you to be my wife."

Chapter 2

Ainsley stared at Santiago, certain she had misunderstood. Surely he wasn't really suggesting she play his wife for his little sting operation?

"Excuse me?"

His green gaze didn't waver. "I said I want you to be my wife. You're the only one who I can trust to help me with this."

So he was serious.

The initial shock faded as anger bubbled to the surface. The nerve of this man! To sit here in her office and casually suggest she play his wife, when he'd walked out on her five years ago, claiming he wasn't the marrying kind! It was a cruel joke; even he had to know that.

She shook her head. "That's not funny."

"I'm not joking," he said calmly. "I meant what I said, Ainsley. I trust you."

"Find someone else," she said flatly, determined not to let her emotions show.

"There is no one else," he replied.

"Don't you have a girlfriend who could do the job?"

He shook his head, opened his mouth to speak again. But she cut him off. "Hire someone, then."

"It's not the same," he said. Santiago leaned forward, his expression earnest. "I know this is awkward."

Ainsley snorted, and he had the grace to look embarrassed. "Believe me, I wouldn't ask you if it wasn't so important."

"I still don't understand why you can't hire someone. I'm sure there's at least one underworked actress in Phoenix looking for some extra cash."

"I'm sure there is, too," he replied. "But you and I have a history together. An intimacy that can't be faked. The people running the retreat aren't stupid. They'll know in an instant if I bring an actress with me. But you…" He trailed off, tipped his head to the side. "You know me."

It was true—she did. They'd met in law school and quickly become inseparable. She'd loved him with all her heart, had spent hours imagining their lives together, dreaming of what things would be like. She couldn't have children thanks to a childhood surgery that had resulted in massive internal scarring, leaving her infertile. Santiago knew that, and he'd assured her that wasn't a problem for him, that he didn't want kids. Everything had seemed so perfect—their future bright. She'd given him years, only to be cast aside so he could move to New York and become a big shot.

A part of her had always wondered if he'd told the truth. Had he really left to chase his professional dreams? Or had he wanted to find a woman who could give him children, in case he changed his mind later?

It was a question that still haunted Ainsley from time to time. She'd had years to accept the fact that she would never be pregnant, never have a baby come from her body. There were moments she still grieved the loss of possibility, but she'd made her peace with it. If she ever decided she had to be a mother, she'd look into adoption. Perhaps Santiago hadn't felt the same way. Maybe that had turned out to be a deal-breaker after all, despite his words to the contrary.

Eventually, Ainsley had decided it didn't matter. Whatever his motivations, he was gone from her life. She'd tried to move on, and for the most part, she'd done so successfully.

But now he was back, pouring salt in the wounds he'd inflicted, wearing an apologetic smile and shrugging as if to say, "What can I do?"

Why did he have to look so damn handsome, too? His charcoal suit fit him to perfection, and his crisp white button-down was open at the collar, providing a tantalizing glimpse of his golden tan skin. She knew from experience how warm he was, how solid he felt pressed up against her body. How he could read her moods with just a glance, know exactly what she needed from him at any given moment. He'd felt like an extension of her soul, and when he'd left she'd felt like her world had shifted overnight, never to be the same again. And just like the earthquake that had rocked Mustang Valley a few months ago, Santiago's departure had left permanent marks on her heart.

"Please, Ainsley," he said. His voice was low, but there was a subtle note of anxiety that cut through her anger. "I'm not trying to hurt you again. But I need you."

She knew how much the admission cost him. Santiago's pride ran deep, and he'd always hated to ask for help. It was a big deal for him to admit he needed her now.

But he was also asking for a huge favor.

Ainsley sighed, considering her options. Like it or not, she needed Santiago. Or rather, Ace needed Santiago. If she refused to play a part in his undercover operation, he might very well walk out of her office and leave her and her brother high and dry. It seemed the only way she was going to be able to help Ace was if she pushed aside her feelings and helped the man who'd broken her heart.

"All right," she said finally.

Relief flashed across his face and the breath

gusted out of him. Ainsley was a little surprised at his reaction—apparently, he hadn't taken her agreement for granted.

"Thank you," he said. He moved his hands as though he wanted to reach across the desk and touch her, but stopped short of the gesture. "I can't tell you how much I appreciate this."

"Don't thank me yet," she cautioned. "This plan of yours might not work."

"It will. I know it will." He got to his feet, all traces of vulnerability gone as his confident facade slipped back into place. "I'm going to call and make the appointment at the center. I'm hoping to get in this weekend, and the retreat lasts a week. Will that work for your schedule?"

Ainsley stood and made a show of checking her calendar, though she knew it would be fine. "All right," she said. "I can clear some time."

"Excellent." Santiago smiled at her, flashing the dimples that never failed to make women sigh. "I will contact your brother. I should be able to make some headway on his case before our session at the center."

"Use my middle name and your fake surname when you register us," she said.

Santiago tilted his head to the side. "Grace Rodriguez?"

Ainsley nodded. "This place is close to Mustang Valley, so there's a chance people working there might recognize the name Ainsley Colton. If you want this sham to work, you'd better use my middle name so no one questions our relationship."

Santiago nodded. "Good idea. I was going to use a different last name, just to make sure no one connected me with my sister. That will also provide an extra layer of coverage for you as well."

He turned to go, moving across the room with that smooth gait she knew so well. "Santiago," she called, just before he reached the door.

At the sound of his name, Santiago stopped and looked back. "Yes?"

There was just one thing she had to know before he left. "If I had said no, would you still have taken my brother's case?" Was this simply a quid pro quo arrangement? Or would he have helped regardless of her answer?

He didn't hesitate. "Of course." He studied her for a few seconds, his gaze probing. "I once told you I would always be there for you. I meant it."

Ainsley sucked in a breath as a tingle shot down her spine. He'd said those words to her just before he'd moved to New York. At the time, she'd thought he was simply trying to make her feel better, to make it seem that even though he was blowing up her dreams of a future together, he still wanted to be friends.

Apparently, he'd been making a promise.

She nodded, her throat too tight to speak. Damn him! This would have been easier if he'd kept things transactional—a you scratch my back, I'll scratch yours kind of thing. But he had to go and bring up his parting words, stirring up all kinds of emotions she'd thought were long buried.

Santiago's expression changed, a knowing look entering his eyes. For a second, she thought he was going to come back, to embrace her the way he'd always done in the past when she'd been upset. But he stayed by the door, apparently recognizing it wasn't his place to comfort her anymore.

He offered her a small nod. "I'll be in touch."

Ainsley tried to smile. "Great," she replied, trying to sound casual. "I'll clear my schedule starting on Friday for the next week."

He inclined his head in a nod of acknowledgment. Then he turned and walked out of her office.

Ainsley waited until the door shut behind him before dropping back into her chair. Seeing Santiago again had been challenging—he was still handsome, still charming.

Still her missing piece.

She shook her head, dismissing the romantic notion. She didn't need anyone to complete her. She was a strong, intelligent woman who had friends and family who loved her and a career she enjoyed. She wasn't broken or somehow less than simply because she was single.

But there were times when she was lonely.

Once upon a time, Santiago had felt like her other half. He'd been her safe place, the person she went to when she had joys to share or sorrows to grieve.

He'd always been there for her, a steadfast, constant presence that she'd thought would always be part of her life. When he'd left, she had mourned as though he'd died. It had taken years, but she'd gotten to the point where she didn't think of him every day anymore, didn't feel that hollow ache in the center of her chest whenever something reminded her of him.

Now that she'd seen him again though, she felt bruised. All her hard work, all the time and energy she'd put into moving on—it wasn't enough. It was like the past five years hadn't happened, and she was back at square one, feeling raw and vulnerable and exposed all over again.

Playing the part of Santiago's wife would be a particularly ironic job since he'd left her because he hadn't wanted to commit. In the weeks after he'd moved, she'd sometimes fantasized about him coming back, metaphorical hat in hand, realizing he'd been wrong to let her go. He'd get down on his knees and beg her to take him back, plead for her forgiveness and grovel for his shortsighted mistake. The fantasy had helped her feel better, even though she'd known it would never happen.

And yet, in a strange twist of fate, he'd returned. Although he hadn't groveled, he did need her help.

At least this time, she knew the score from the beginning.

"It's business," she muttered to herself. "Only a business arrangement." No matter how personal it seemed, she had to remember that she was playing a part. Yes, they shared a past. But they didn't have a future together. She would do this favor for him, he would help her brother, and then they'd part ways and go back to their separate lives.

For a split second, she thought about backing out. Santiago had said he'd still help Ace even if she didn't help him. Why put herself through the emotional wringer if she didn't absolutely have to?

But she dismissed the idea with her next breath. If she didn't help Santiago, she'd feel like she owed him for taking Ace's case. At least this way, they were balanced. A few days of awkwardness was preferable to being indebted to Santiago.

And maybe in some ways this would be good for her. She'd spent so much time mourning what might have been, she'd lost sight of all the reasons why she and Santiago might not have worked out to begin with. All his annoying traits had faded into the recesses of her memories. Perhaps a reminder of his imperfections and bad habits was just what she needed to realize how lucky she was to still be single.

Ainsley straightened, warming to the thought. It was the perfect approach to take for this upcoming ordeal. Instead of focusing on what she'd lost, she'd think about what she'd avoided and what she had now. Best of all, it would help her keep Santiago at arm's length, which was what she needed to do for both her heart and the purposes of his ruse. It would be a win-win-win all around. Ace would get the best defense lawyer in the state; Santiago would help his sister; and she would have a renewed appreciation for her life.

She took a deep breath, recalling her interrupted meditation session earlier in the day. Everything would go back to normal soon. She just had to get through this first.

Friday morning.

"More coffee?"

Santiago glanced up at the waitress, who stood next to the table holding a full carafe. "Yes, please." He lifted his cup to make it easier for her to pour, then brought the brew to his face to inhale the fragrant steam. Bubba's Diner wasn't the fanciest place in town, but the coffee was hot and the pancakes were fluffy.

"You ready to order yet?"

"Another moment, please," Santiago said with a smile. "I'm sure my friend will be here shortly."

The waitress nodded and walked off to attend another table. Santiago glanced at his watch. Ace Colton was late.

He added a packet of sugar and a dollop of cream to his coffee, then stirred gently. Just as he brought the mug to his lips the door to the diner opened, setting a string of bells jingling.

Ace walked inside and stopped just past the threshold. Santiago threw up his arm and gave him a little wave, and Ace nodded.

"Sorry I'm late," he said as he slid into the booth across from Santiago. "I had a rough night."

He looked it, too, with his tousled hair, stubbled cheeks and red-rimmed eyes.

"I understand," Santiago said, offering his hand. It was the truth—he hadn't slept well either, but for different reasons. Seeing Ainsley again had been a shock to his system. He'd assumed the passage of time would have dulled his body's response to her, but he'd been wrong. He'd spent last night tossing and turning, wanting nothing more than to go back to her office and lay her back on that wide desk of hers. Or the coffee table he'd spied in the sitting area. Or any flat surface, really. He wasn't picky. He just ached to feel her again, to have her in his arms once more.

Ace shook his hand, pulling him out of his thoughts. "I remember you." His gaze turned assessing. "You dumped my sister to chase your career." He tilted his head to the side. "How'd that work out for you?"

Guilt speared Santiago's heart, but he ignored the uncomfortable sensation. "Depends on your perspective," he said, deliberately keeping his tone light. He wasn't about to get into the details of his past with Ainsley with her brother, and especially not here.

Ace studied him a moment, and Santiago got the impression the other man was debating on staying or going. "Ainsley says you're the best," he said finally.

Pleasure bloomed in Santiago's chest. It meant

a lot to know that despite their past, Ainsley still thought highly of his professional skills and trusted him to defend her brother. "I'm glad she called me." *For more reasons than one.* "I think I can help you."

A look of relief flashed across Ace's face. "I trust my sister's judgment. If she thinks you're good, I do, too."

Smart man. Santiago knew from experience Ainsley had a brilliant legal mind. She'd had her pick of firms, but her loyalty to her family had led her to choose corporate law and Colton Oil.

"Ainsley told me about your situation. But I'd like to hear the details from you, if you don't mind." Santiago liked to hear his clients tell their stories firsthand, as often their body language and facial expressions told him just as much as their words.

Ace nodded, then started talking, pausing only to place an order for food and coffee when the waitress stopped by the table again. He told Santiago about the initial email and the board's reaction, the DNA test and Payne Colton's response to finding out Ace wasn't his biological son. Ace tried to hide it, but it was clear from the anguish in his eyes that Payne's actions had hurt him deeply.

He expressed shock over Payne's shooting, and even more disbelief at the fact the police had found a gun in his condo yesterday.

"It's not mine, I swear it," Ace said, leaning forward for emphasis. "I don't know where it came from, but someone must have planted it."

Santiago nodded, jotting down notes on a small pad. "Does anyone else have a key to your condo?"

Ace shook his head, but then stopped and frowned. "The cleaning lady," he said. "And maybe the property management company?" He sounded uncertain about the last possibility.

"Let's start with the cleaning lady first," Santiago replied. "What's her name?"

Ace rattled off the information, and Santiago dutifully recorded her name and number. "Any security tapes?" he asked.

"I do have some cameras installed inside," Ace said. "And I know the building has some security cameras."

"All right. I'll want to see the footage from your cameras," Santiago said.

"I can email the files to you, but the police already looked at everything," Ace said. He sounded discouraged. "They said they didn't find anything."

Santiago smiled. "They may not have found evidence of a crime, but I have a different set of criteria for evaluation."

Ace considered that for a second. "I like it," he said, nodding slowly.

"What about this source? What did the police say her name was again?"

"Destiny Jones." Ace practically spat the name. "I have no idea who she is."

"The police told you she said she'd seen the gun during an intimate encounter?"

"Yeah. Except I've never seen the woman, much less slept with her!"

Santiago tilted his head to the side. "This is only going to work if you're 100 percent honest with me." He had to know everything about Ace's actions over the past few months, even the details that might be considered embarrassing.

Ace's eyes widened. "I'm telling you the truth! I have no idea who she is. She could walk right up to me and I wouldn't know her."

"Okay." He decided to take Ace at his word. The man didn't appear to be lying; in fact, the whole time he'd been talking he'd seemed genuine and sincere. It was still possible Santiago was being played, but if that was the case, Ace Colton was a terrific actor.

"Any chance you know her by a different name?"

Ace shook his head. "How would I know that?"

Santiago took a sip of coffee. "I'm asking you if you've taken a woman back to your condo for personal reasons. Maybe someone you don't know very well, or only just met? A professional, perhaps?" Ace looked aghast, so Santiago held up a hand. "I'm not here to judge you. I'm just trying to find out if this woman got inside your condo by pretending to be someone else."

"That's not possible," Ace said flatly. "I'm not in a relationship, and I don't need to pay for companionship. The only woman who has regular access to my place is the maid, and Maria has worked for me for years. I doubt she'd do something like this."

"Fair enough," Santiago said easily. "Let's switch gears. Who found Payne after he'd been shot?" He hadn't had time to pull the police reports this morning before coming to the diner. It was on his to-do list, but given the time crunch he was facing, he'd decided to prioritize talking to Ace and hearing his side of things. He wanted to gather as much information as possible before Saturday, when he and Ainsley had their appointment at The Marriage Institute. The two of them were going to have to share a room for the duration of the retreat, and bringing a pile of work was a surefire way to keep both his hands and his mind occupied.

"The Colton Oil cleaning lady found him," Ace said. "Her name is Joanne Bates. She's worked for the company for the past five years. I don't have her contact information with me, but I know Ainsley can get you her number."

Santiago nodded. "Sounds good."

The waitress delivered their food. Santiago asked Ace a few more questions between bites of pancakes and eggs, getting to know the man's temperament. He'd done some online research last night and had learned from several industry articles that Ace had a reputation as a ruthless businessman.

"Have you ever double-crossed someone in a deal?"

Ace shrugged. "I'm sure it probably felt that way to some people, but I'm always careful to do things by the book. My actions are always legal, even though they might not be nice."

"Can you think of anyone who would want to frame you for Payne's attempted murder? Any enemies in your personal or business life who want to see you suffer?"

Ace took a bite of bacon and chewed, his expression thoughtful. "Not off the top of my head," he said. "I've been thinking about it since yesterday, when the cops found that gun. Ainsley thinks maybe someone is trying to get me back for a business deal gone wrong, but I can't come up with any people who would feel that way." He took a sip of coffee and shrugged. "The people I deal with all know the score. I do what's necessary to advance my company. They're the same way." A shadow crossed his face. "At least, it *was* my company."

Santiago felt a pang of sympathy for the guy. It had to be hard, losing his job, his family, his identity all at the same time.

They finished up and Santiago signaled for the check. He had a lot of work ahead of him, and the sooner he got started, the better.

"Thanks for meeting me on such short notice," he said as he signed the credit card receipt.

"Of course," Ace said. "I appreciate you taking my case."

"I'll probably have some more questions for you," Santiago said. "I know the police already told you this, but you need to stay in town. Don't give them a reason to suspect you more than they already do."

Ace nodded. "I know. I'm just tired of getting blamed for something I didn't do."

"I can understand that," Santiago replied. "And I'll do my best to prove you're not the one who shot Payne."

They stood and headed for the door. "Let me know what you need from me," Ace said, shaking Santiago's hand once they'd stepped outside. "Anything I can do to help you, I will."

"Thank you," Santiago said. "I'll be in touch."

They parted ways, and Santiago glanced down the street. The police department was only a few blocks away, at the end of Mustang Boulevard. The sun was bright, but the heat of the day had yet to settle over the town. A walk would help him organize his thoughts, so he set off in the direction of the one-story brick building.

He walked past a few storefronts, his mind ticking through options and making a mental to-do list. A kid on a bicycle careened toward him, so he stepped to the side to let the child pass. The move brought him up against the display windows of a jewelry store, and he was confronted by the sight of dozens of diamond rings, all sparkling in the sun.

Santiago's stomach dropped as he realized he needed to buy Ainsley—and himself—rings. They were supposed to be married, after all, and married people wore wedding bands. But would she do that for him? Or was that taking things one step too far?

He remained rooted to the spot, indecision keeping him from walking away but also preventing him from going into the store. They would make a more convincing couple if they had wedding rings. If he'd hired a woman to play the part of his wife, he wouldn't hesitate to supply the necessary prop. But Ainsley wasn't just any woman. And this wouldn't be just any ring.

Santiago shook his head, wishing for the millionth time there had been some way to preserve their relationship. But given his own dismal family history where love was concerned, he'd known his best option was to focus all his energy on his career and making a name for himself. At least he'd have some fulfillment in his life, even though legal briefs didn't exactly keep him warm at night.

There had been times he'd questioned his decision. But in those moments of doubt, he'd only had to think of his parents and their seemingly permanent state of misery to know he'd made the right choice. His actions had paid off, at least professionally. He'd done well for himself career-wise. And he hadn't lacked for company on a personal level. But he'd never truly connected with anyone the way he had with Ainsley. His relationships had been pleasant but superficial, and he'd been careful to ensure that the women he'd dated didn't get the wrong idea about a future with him.

He simply wasn't the marrying kind.

The men in his family were cursed when it came to marriage. He'd never met his grandparents, but his father had told him how unhappy they'd been together. And his own parents had made no secret of their disdain for each other. It was still a mystery to him why his parents had stayed together, but Gabriela had once told him she thought their mother and father wouldn't separate because they hated each other too much to want to risk the other finding happiness with someone else. It made a sick kind of sense—they were locked in a self-destructive cycle, where punishing each other was more important than their own joy.

Growing up, Santiago had simply assumed he'd be alone. But when he'd met Ainsley in law school, he hadn't been able to stay away from her. She was totally unlike his mother, her opposite in practically every way. Ainsley had taught him that relationships didn't have to be prisons of misery, that both people could and should be happy together. And they had been, for a while.

But as the years had passed, Santiago had known Ainsley wanted to settle down. She'd made no secret of her desire for marriage, just as he'd been upfront about the fact that he wasn't marriage material. When the job in New York had come up, he'd jumped at the chance to leave. Better to break it off while they still liked each other than let their affections wither and die because he couldn't give her what she wanted most. No way was he going to follow in his parents' footsteps.

He'd never thought he would be in the position of picking out a wedding ring. And yet here he was, standing outside a jewelry store and checking out the sparkling display.

A small part of him was curious about the process. Ainsley was the only woman in his life he might even imagine marrying, so it was somehow fitting he needed to pick out a wedding set for her. But not a diamond. Diamonds were significant—they meant commitment, a white dress, the whole nine yards. No, he needed something more subtle. Something that would look nice, but that wouldn't send her mixed signals. He knew she wasn't happy about doing him this favor, and he couldn't blame her. He'd broken her heart five years ago, was lucky she'd even agreed to speak with him. Buying her a diamond ring and asking her to wear it would just be cruel, and he never wanted to hurt her.

Santiago peered past the window display, trying to see deeper into the store. Surely they carried more than just diamonds?

Only one way to find out. With a sigh, he pulled open the door and stepped inside.

Chapter 3

Still at the office?

Ainsley read Santiago's text later that day and frowned. Yes, she was working late. But she wasn't really in the mood to talk right now.

Yes, she wrote back. Big project.

His reply was swift. Excellent. Be right there.

"Oh, come on," she muttered. Was he really going to barge into her office on such short notice two days in a row? She was grateful he'd taken Ace's case, but she had her limits.

Ten minutes later, there was a knock on her door.

She got to her feet and headed across the office, stopping for a second as she caught a glimpse of herself in the mirror on the wall. Her hair looked a bit frazzled, and her blouse was wrinkled. She couldn't fix her shirt, but she did a quick U-turn and snagged an elastic band off her desk. Working quickly, she smoothed her hair back into a short ponytail. Then she shrugged into her blazer, hoping it would hide the wrinkles. It was silly, she knew, but she wanted to look good in front of Santiago. Let him see what he'd been missing over the years. Her pride demanded nothing less.

He smiled when she opened the door, those dimples making an appearance once more. "Thanks for seeing me."

She arched a brow and stepped aside so he could enter. "You didn't give me much choice."

He chuckled, the low sound going straight to her belly. "That's true, I didn't." He held up a large paper bag as he walked past her. "Do you still like orange chicken?"

Ainsley caught a whiff of the hot Chinese food and her mouth watered. She was trying to cram in as much work as possible before the retreat, so she'd skipped lunch thanks to back-to-back meetings. The granola bar she'd snagged a few hours ago was a distant memory to her empty stomach.

"I do," she replied, restraining the urge to wrest the bag from his grasp. "But you didn't have to bring dinner." It was a thoughtful gesture. It also stung a little. How many nights had they spent together, poring over legal texts while munching on pizza or other takeout?

Santiago shrugged and placed the bag on the conference table set up on the right side of the office. "I needed to talk to you, and I'm hungry. Thought you might be, too. This seemed like the most efficient use of our time."

She couldn't fault his logic. Ainsley gathered paper plates from the cabinet next to the table and joined him as he removed box after box of food from the bag.

"I got a little of everything," he explained, pointing to each carton as he named the contents.

Ainsley took an egg roll. "Any mustard sauce?" she asked hopefully.

Santiago reached into the bag and pulled out a few packets with a grin. "Of course," he said. "I know better than to leave that behind."

Ainsley smiled, feeling a little touched that he'd remembered her preferences after so long apart.

They dished food onto their plates and for a few minutes, they were both quiet as they focused on those first bites.

"I met your brother this morning," he said after a bite.

"I know." She spoke around a mouthful of chicken and rice. "He called me after."

Santiago smiled at that. "I figured he would. For what it's worth, he thinks highly of your legal skills and judgment."

Ainsley's ego preened. "That's good to know."

"Smart of him," Santiago continued. "You've always been an amazing lawyer."

The unexpected praise caught her by surprise. She sucked in a breath, inhaling a grain of rice. Her throat spasmed, triggering a fit of coughing that caused her to lean forward in her chair.

"Are you okay?" Santiago looked alarmed, and he set his fork down. Ainsley waved away his concern, but she couldn't stop coughing. Santiago stood up and crouched next to her, placing his large hand flat on her back. He started to gently rub circles between her shoulder blades, leaning in close as though his proximity could help her.

Gradually, the coughing subsided. Santiago leaned over and grabbed a bottle of water off the counter of the low cabinets. He twisted off the cap and handed it to her, then resumed rubbing circles on her back.

Ainsley took a cautious sip, relieved when it didn't trigger a new coughing fit. "Thanks," she said, turning to look at him. "I think I'm good now." Her voice sounded a little hoarse, belying her words.

He was close enough that she could see the thin ring of gold that circled his pupils. His eyes had always reminded her of green turquoise, the color almost too beautiful to be real.

The breath caught in her throat as he leaned in, his gaze intent on hers. She was acutely aware of his touch on her back. The warmth of his body heated the space between them, and she had the sudden urge to press herself to him, to flatten her curves against his solid chest and breathe in his intoxicating scent. His pheromones were better than any drug, and their effects as potent now as they'd ever been. She'd already overcome that particular addiction once. If she wasn't careful, she'd get hooked again.

"Are you sure you're all right?"

Ainsley nodded, not trusting her voice.

Santiago held her gaze a few seconds more, assessing her condition for himself. Apparently convinced she was telling the truth, he leaned back and placed his hand on the table as he stood.

Ainsley immediately felt the loss of his touch. She looked away as he sat in his chair again, hoping her disappointment didn't show.

Get it together! she silently chided herself. She'd spent a grand total of an hour or so in Santiago's presence over the last twenty-four hours, and she was already melting for him again. How was she going to survive this marriage retreat if she couldn't keep her emotions and body in check?

"So what did you think of Ace?" Change the subject, focus on something else. By engaging her mind, maybe she could forget about the effect he was having on her body...

Santiago tilted his head to the side as he pinched a bit of chicken between his chopsticks. "I think he's telling the truth."

Some of the knots in Ainsley's chest loosened at

his words. "I think so, too," she confessed. "But part of me was worried I wasn't thinking clearly because he's my brother—even if not biologically. It's good to know you have the same impression."

Santiago shot her a grin. "Always trust your instincts," he advised. "I asked him a lot of questions this morning. I could tell by the way he answered that he was being truthful—he didn't prevaricate, or hesitate to respond. And his words didn't sound rehearsed, either."

"This has been hard on him," Ainsley said. A shadow passed over her heart as she thought about the events of the last several months. It felt like her family was coming apart at the seams, and no matter how hard she tried, she couldn't fix everything.

"I don't think he's the only one having trouble," Santiago said softly. She looked up to find him watching her, his expression kind.

She smiled absently and pushed away her thoughts. "It's been a shock to us all," she said, striving to make her tone light. If he kept looking at her like that, she was going to break down and cry. And while Santiago had once been her safe harbor, she had to remember he wasn't anymore.

"I spoke with the police after I talked to Ace," he said, smoothly steering the conversation away from troubled waters. "One of the officers was helpful. Spencer Colton was his name—another family member?"

"A cousin," Ainsley confirmed. "I'm glad he was cooperative."

"Very," Santiago said. "He put me in touch with the D.A.'s office, and they gave me the names and contact information of the witnesses in the case. I've already made appointments to speak to your brother's housekeeper and the cleaner who discovered your father."

Ainsley nodded. "That was fast."

"No point in waiting," he said. "Besides, you're helping me out for the next week. I wanted to make a good faith effort on your brother's case, so you wouldn't think I was taking advantage of your co-operation."

"I know you wouldn't do that." It was true. She might not be able to trust him with her heart, but she knew he was a man of his word. He'd told her he'd represent Ace. There was no doubt in her mind that he would follow through.

"I, uh, did want to talk to you about the retreat." He shifted in his seat, looking uncharacteristically uncertain.

Interesting, she thought. Perhaps Santiago was having second thoughts about his plan? Maybe she wouldn't have to spend the next seven days pretending to be the wife of the man who'd broken her heart?

"All right." She pushed her plate away, no longer hungry. "We should probably come up with a strategy. Make sure we're on the same page."

He nodded. "I'm working on an email that outlines everything. I'll finish it tonight and send it to you. We can talk about any questions you have in the car tomorrow, on the way to the retreat."

Ainsley's stomach did a little flip-flop. They were really going to do this. It was time for her to fulfill her promise.

"I'll look for it later," she said. She was curious to know what Santiago had in mind and how he was going to get the information he needed to prove The Marriage Institute was scamming people. But she hoped she'd be able to keep a professional distance from him while they worked.

"There's one more thing." He looked down, clearly uncomfortable. A stone of dread formed in Ainsley's stomach. Was he going to change the deal? Did he need her to do more than just pretend to be his wife?

"I did a little shopping today," he continued. He sighed, then withdrew something from his jacket pocket. He placed it on the table, exactly in the middle of the space separating them.

Ainsley stared at the small black velvet box as though it were a bomb. She glanced up and Santiago offered her a shrug and a slight wince. "I just thought..." he trailed off. "I mean, we *are* supposed to be married."

She shook her head, not knowing whether to laugh or to cry. How many times had she dreamed of this man giving her a ring? How many times had she fantasized about him proposing to her? How he'd look, how he'd sound. How the love he had for her would shine on his face as he asked her to spend the rest of her life with him. And the joy that she'd feel, the unmitigated happiness she'd experience when he slipped the ring on her finger, a tangible symbol of their commitment to each other.

Instead, she was sitting in her office, her dinner forming a cold lump in her stomach while Santiago had trouble meeting her eyes.

She reached for the box without conscious thought. Might as well get this over with.

The ring was beautiful. A round emerald surrounded by a halo of tiny diamonds sat on a thin band of white gold. Additional small diamonds decorated the sides of the band. Even in the soft light of her office, she could see the stone was a deep, verdant green, the color of summer grass. The diamonds sparkled like tiny stars, making the ring glitter as though lit from within. There was a thin wedding band nestled under the ring, carved with an intricate scroll filigree that was exquisitely delicate.

Ainsley swallowed hard, trying to keep her emotions at bay. "It's lovely," she said, her heart aching as she stared at it.

Santiago cleared his throat. "Under the circumstances, I didn't think a big diamond would be appropriate."

"No," she agreed, tearing her gaze away to meet his eyes. "This is fine."

"I had to pick something that looked like a wedding set," he said, sounding nervous. "This wasn't being sold as an engagement ring, but when I saw the emerald, I thought it was fitting."

"Your family," she murmured. Santiago's parents were from Colombia, a country famous for its emeralds.

"Exactly." He looked relieved that she understood. "And then I saw the thin band, and I thought they looked good together."

If the circumstances were different, Ainsley would have sworn Santiago was worried about her liking the rings. "They're very nice," she said. Her fingers were stiff as she pulled the rings from the box and slid them on. They fit perfectly. Of course.

"I had to guess your size," he said, watching her movements. "Looks like I got it right."

"You did," she said flatly. Ainsley stared at her left hand for a moment, trying to adjust to the sight of the jewelry. It looked like a stranger's hand, one she'd never seen before.

The surreal image was too much. She tugged the rings off and put them back in the box, feeling shaken.

"You don't have to wear them," Santiago said hastily. "It's fine if you'd rather not."

She shook her head. "No, I'll do it." He wasn't the only one who kept promises. She'd told him she would pretend to be his wife for the retreat. "What about you?" she asked. "Do I need to find a band for you?" Just the thought of walking into a jewelry store to buy Santiago a wedding band was enough to make her heart hurt, but she'd play her part.

"No," he said emphatically. He stuck his hand into his pocket again and held up a gold ring. "I'm all set."

Ainsley nodded, relief stealing over her. "What time are we leaving tomorrow?"

Santiago returned the band to his pocket. "I was thinking we could go around four. That way we can both get some work done and it won't be a totally wasted day."

"That works for me." She stood and began to gather up the remains of their meal. She needed him to leave now, needed to be alone so she could process her feelings in private and get her emotions locked down before the retreat started. The wedding rings had been an unexpected surprise, and she wasn't sure how she felt about them.

Apparently recognizing his cue, Santiago pushed back in his chair and helped her clean off the table. She left the small velvet box alone, not ready to touch it again just yet.

"Where should I pick you up tomorrow?" he asked. "Here at the office, or at your home?"

"Here is fine," she replied. She didn't want him coming to the house she shared with her siblings and father. She might have her own wing of rooms, but the house was never empty. If anyone saw him there they'd have questions, and she wasn't in the mood to provide answers. Besides, the last thing she wanted was to have Santiago in her private living quarters.

His very presence would forever alter the character of the space, and she'd feel like a stranger in her own home. The rooms were her escape from the demands of her career and her family, her safe haven where she could relax and recharge. She didn't need to be haunted by memories of Santiago in her home, examining her personal items and studying the private side of her life.

Santiago nodded, oblivious to her thoughts. "Very good," he said. "I'll come here then."

Before she could react, he took a step forward and leaned down to press a kiss to her cheek. Ainsley sucked in a breath at the contact. Santiago drew back, then froze as their eyes met.

It was clear from the look on his face he'd acted without thinking. She knew she shouldn't read into the gesture, that he'd been moving on autopilot and the kiss had simply been offered out of habit. But her cheek tingled from the contact, and her heart thumped hard against her ribs. With this man, her body wasn't capable of ignoring any contact, no matter how innocent.

Something flashed in his green gaze—heat? Awareness? His eyes dropped to her lips. Unconsciously, her tongue darted out to moisten them. *What are you doing?* she screamed silently to herself. She didn't want to seduce him, didn't want him to think she was interested. But her brain was no longer in charge. Ainsley felt her skin warm as his scent filled her nose—starch, coffee and that intangible note that belonged to him alone.

His head dipped closer, making her breath stutter in her chest. Was he really going to kiss her? More importantly, was she going to stop him?

Apparently not. Without conscious thought, she leaned forward, reducing the distance between them. Santiago smiled faintly, and then she felt the warmth of his mouth as he brushed his lips against her own.

It was a gentle caress, the pressure like the stroke of a butterfly's wings. But it started a fire in her belly that shot tendrils of heat through her limbs and triggered an ache in her heart.

Santiago pulled back, his lips shining and a bewildered look in his eyes.

"I—" He broke off, shaking his head. "I'm sorry," he said finally.

Ainsley took a deep breath, trying to regain her equilibrium. "It's fine," she said. She glanced away, unable to meet his eyes. "I'll see you tomorrow."

Santiago hesitated, then moved away. The tension in her body eased as the distance between them increased. "Yes, of course," he said, his tone professional now, as if he hadn't just kissed her for the first time in more than five years. "Thank you again for your help."

"Likewise," she said. She stood and walked to her desk, placing her hand on it for support. "I appreciate you getting started on Ace's case so quickly."

"It was the least I could do." He paused by the

door, and she got the feeling there was more he wanted to say. But she kept her eyes on her desk, not wanting to engage him further.

He got the hint. She heard him sigh quietly. "Have a good evening."

"You, too," she said automatically. She waited until the door shut behind him before sinking into her desk chair. What had she done?

She rubbed absently at her mouth, her lips still tingling from the contact with his. Twenty-four hours, and she'd already kissed him.

"Technically, he kissed me," she muttered. But that didn't matter. The kiss had happened, and now she was going to have to forget about it.

They had a long week of close contact coming up. She couldn't afford to get distracted, to let her body run the show.

If she was going to get through this with her heart intact, she couldn't let things get personal between them again.

The next afternoon, Santiago pulled into the parking lot in front of the offices of Colton Oil and cut the engine. A quick glance at his watch confirmed he was a little early, so he decided to wait a few minutes before heading up to Ainsley's office.

Nerves crackled in his stomach, making him feel unsettled. It was a strange sensation, one he didn't experience often. He could count on one hand the number of times he'd been nervous in his adult life, and he'd still have fingers left over. What was it about this situation that had him feeling out of sorts?

A flash of light caught his eye and he focused on the gold band on his left hand. The metal gleamed in the afternoon sun, as bright as a flame. He stared at the ring for a moment, having a hard time believing what he was seeing even though he'd put the band on his own finger earlier in the day.

After a childhood spent living in the shadows of his parents' contentious relationship, Santiago had known marriage was not in his future. Even though his relationship with Ainsley had been good—better than he'd ever thought possible—a part of him had always known it wouldn't last. Couldn't last. After all, his own parents had started out madly in love with each other. But somewhere along the way, their affection had withered into mutual contempt. It was a pattern that had been repeated throughout the generations of his family, one he was determined to stop.

So when he'd had an opportunity to move to New York to launch his career after law school, he'd said goodbye to Ainsley, knowing he was really doing her a favor. Better to leave now, while they still liked each other, than to let things disintegrate into the inevitable unpleasantness that would come.

He'd missed her terribly at first. Still did, if he was being honest with himself. Not that he lacked for company. He'd dated several women in New York, all of them beautiful and pleasant. But despite the affection he'd felt for each one, he'd never experienced the soul-deep connection that he'd had with Ainsley. Seeing her again had stirred up latent emotions, feelings he thought he'd processed long ago. But it turned out he'd simply buried his emotions in work rather than deal with them. Now he was going to have to pay the price.

Could he really go through with this? Could he really handle this sham marriage for the week? They'd be living in the same cottage, spending most of their time together. Her scent would be in his nose, her voice in his ears. His body already wanted her again—it had taken all of thirty seconds for his libido to sit up and take notice after walking into her office. And then that moment last night, when he'd kissed her...

It had been the wrong thing to do, he knew that. But it had felt so very right.

"It wasn't even a real kiss," he muttered to himself. No, that had been more like a prelude to a kiss, a teasing promise of things to come. The barest brush of his lips against hers, nothing more.

And yet he'd had to take a cold shower last night before he'd been able to fall asleep.

Santiago shook his head at his own foolishness. Here he was, acting like a randy teenager when really, nothing had happened. To make matters worse, he was certain his feelings were all one-sided. Ainsley had looked shocked after the almost-kiss, but she'd quickly regained her composure. Probably because it wasn't even a blip on her radar. He'd been burning for her after one brief taste, but she'd clearly felt nothing beyond annoyance.

Not that he blamed her. He didn't know why he'd gotten so familiar with her last night. It certainly wasn't something he'd planned. He'd meant to keep things strictly professional between them. But something about that moment had made him forget where they were and what they were doing. He'd gotten distracted by her nearness and the years apart had melted away, making him think they were still together. He'd acted on instinct, moving in to touch her the way he'd done a million times before. Back when he'd still had that privilege.

"It won't happen again," he told himself sternly. It couldn't. He had to expose this marriage retreat for the fraud it was, and the only way to do that was with Ainsley's help. If he messed things up between them, she'd walk away and he wouldn't be able to help his sister, or the other couples who had made the mistake of trusting these people.

"Eyes on the prize," he muttered. This week would be difficult, but he simply had to shove his feelings and attraction to Ainsley to the side so he could focus on the important job ahead.

He reached for the door handle, only to startle as someone rapped on the passenger side window. Ainsley gave him a little wave and he unlocked the door.

She tossed a bag in the back seat, then opened the door and slid in next to him. "Hey," she said. "I saw you from my office window so I decided to come down. Save you a trip up."

He gawked at her, staring at her hair. It was no longer brown—she'd added honey-blonde highlights throughout, changing her appearance completely.

"You look different," he managed.

She reached up and touched her hair. "Yeah, I did it last night. I think it turned out okay, for a home job."

"It looks good." He'd never thought of her as a blonde, but she carried it well.

"Thanks," she said.

"What possessed you to do it?"

She frowned. "I worried people at the retreat might recognize me. This place is pretty close to Mustang Valley, and I didn't want anyone there to see me and doubt our story."

"Good thinking," he said.

"I do occasionally have good ideas," she said, offering a lop-sided smile.

"So, just the one bag?" he asked, glancing back at the small duffel she'd brought.

"Yep," she confirmed. "I pack light."

"That's right, you do," he murmured. "I'd forgotten."

He caught her eye as he turned around and smiled faintly. She glanced away, lifting her hand to push a strand of hair behind her ear.

Santiago sucked in a breath as he saw the rings on her finger. A shock went through him, an electric zap down his spine that radiated through his limbs. She was wearing the emerald he'd given her.

It shouldn't have been a surprise—she had said she would wear the wedding set. Logically, he'd known he'd see the rings on her finger.

But there was something about the sight of his ring on her left hand that hit him hard. A wave of possessiveness washed over him, his thoughts congealing into a single word: *mine.*

The rational part of his brain recognized he was being ridiculous. The rings were a fake symbol, a prop for the roles they were playing. But some caveman impulse deep inside of him swelled with pleasure to see Ainsley sporting a visible sign of their connection. The whole world would know at a glance that this woman was taken, that she was his.

Even though it wasn't true.

"Are you all right?"

She was studying him with a concerned expression, clearly worried. What must he look like to elicit that question?

Santiago cleared his throat and schooled his features into a neutral mask. "I'm fine. Just thinking about this week."

Ainsley nodded, apparently satisfied by his response. "I'm worried, too. What do you think it will be like?"

He shifted the car into gear and pulled onto the road, starting their journey toward The Marriage Institute retreat center. "Gabriela told me there's a lot of group sessions. For most of them, the husband goes to one, while the wife goes to another."

"They must separate the couples according to who they've rigged to 'win,'" Ainsley said. "How do they decide that?"

"Bribery," Santiago replied. "Has to be."

"It's always about money," she muttered.

Santiago nodded. She'd apparently been thinking about what he'd said, and he appreciated she was taking this seriously. Though he wasn't surprised—he knew from experience that Ainsley Colton was a woman of her word.

"Makes sense," he said. "I have one of my research assistants digging into their financial records. It seems the Woods have some off-shore accounts, which in and of itself isn't so suspicious. But it definitely raises questions."

"You think they've got a tax shelter?"

"Probably," he said. "Once we gather our evidence, I'm hoping the D.A. will be able to open a case and pry into those secrets."

Ainsley was quiet a moment. "So what else should we expect from this thing?"

"Gabriela said there were some joint counseling sessions, but looking back on it, she sees now they were one-sided."

"Like she was being manipulated?" Ainsley asked.

"Exactly," Santiago confirmed. "She said it felt

like the counselor and her husband were a team, and she was on the outside."

"Oh, man." From the edges of his vision, he saw Ainsley shake her head. "That's terrible. I feel so bad for her. Not to mention the rest of the innocent people who went there looking for help. Do you think they took bribes from everybody?"

"Probably not," Santiago said. "But I think they're probably known in certain circles for helping people get the result they want."

"Rich people, you mean," she muttered.

"Yeah," he said. Anger simmered on a low boil in his chest, a sensation he'd felt ever since Gabriela had come to him in tears, confessing her worries and asking him for help. "It makes me sick to think of what these people have done."

"They won't get away with it for much longer," Ainsley said quietly. "We'll make sure of that."

His spirits lifted at her use of the word *we*. It was good to know he wasn't in this alone, despite the personal issues still lurking between them.

"I think the best way to do this is for both of us to offer them a bribe, separately. We'll see if they accept the money."

"Are we offering them the same amount?"

Santiago shook his head. "No. Your envelope has two thousand dollars, with the promise of three thousand more after the retreat is over, provided you get what you want. My bribe will be four thousand dollars, with the promise of six thousand more after the retreat is over."

Ainsley whistled softly. "That's a lot of cash."

"It is," he agreed. "Hopefully too much for them to pass up."

"What about other evidence?" she asked. "Taking bribes is unethical, but it might not be enough to shut this place down."

"That's true," he said. "Which is why we're going to record everything."

He glanced over in time to see her wrinkle her nose. "Is that legal?"

"Technically speaking, yes," he said. "Arizona is a single-party consent state, so as long as you and I know the conversations are being recorded, we're in the clear."

"That's true, so long as the other parties don't have a reasonable expectation of privacy," Ainsley pointed out. "I'm fine with recording our conversations with the Woodses, since they're the ones running this thing and scamming people. But I'm not comfortable recording any of the group counseling sessions. Those other people don't deserve to have their privacy violated like that."

Santiago smiled, enjoying the display of both her intellect and her moral code. He'd definitely picked the right woman to help him bring these charlatans down.

"I totally agree with you," he said. "I wasn't planning on having us record any group counseling sessions. But I do want to record our private sessions with them, and any one-on-one conversations we have with either of them."

She nodded, accepting his response. "I suppose we'll just use our phones?"

"Better," he said. "I have some devices for us to wear." Keeping one hand on the wheel, he reached into the back of the car and grabbed his leather messenger bag. He placed it in Ainsley's lap. "You'll find a flat white box inside," he said.

She hesitated a second, then opened the bag and began to rummage inside. A faint tingle tickled the base of his spine. Seeing Ainsley riffle through his bag felt intimate somehow, though there was really nothing personal inside. The contents were all work-related. If it had been any other person, he would have worried about breaking attorney-client privilege. But he trusted Ainsley and knew she wouldn't examine anything other than the box he'd described.

A few seconds later she withdrew the item in question. "Is this it?"

"That's the one."

She opened the lid and he glanced over to see her press her lips together in a thin line. "More jewelry," she said flatly.

He winced, wishing there had been another option. "I know," he said, his tone apologetic. "But it was my only option."

"It's fine," she said. She studied the necklace, one brow lifted. "Not really my style, but that's all right."

"Believe it or not, that was the best one." Santiago shook his head as he recalled the truly garish pieces he'd seen while searching the internet for something for Ainsley to wear.

She pulled the pendant from the box and clasped the chain around her neck. The silver locket hung just above the neckline of her shirt, perfectly positioned to capture the activity around her. The scrollwork design on the front of the pendant was a bit ostentatious, but it did a good job of disguising the small opening for the camera lens.

"If anyone asks, you can tell them it's a family heirloom," he suggested.

"That works," she said. "It does have an old-fashioned look to it."

"It's touch activated," he told her. "You just have to slide your finger over the surface of the locket to start recording."

"That seems easy enough," she said. She fiddled with it for a few seconds, then placed her hands in her lap again.

"So what's our story?"

He frowned, not entirely sure what she was asking. "Pardon?"

"You know. Why are we there? Why is our marriage in trouble? We've got to have a good reason for wanting to split up."

"Oh." He'd sent her an email earlier with some options for their cover story. Now it seemed they needed to decide what they were going to say.

"I work too much," he said. "No time for the relationship."

She laughed. The sound was unexpected, and it made him smile. "What? Doesn't that sound convincing?"

"Oh, completely," Ainsley said, humor in her voice. "But what about me? Is there any reason you're unhappy with me?"

No, he thought automatically. But he shrugged. "You work a lot, too?" he suggested.

"I think we can do better than that," she said. She was silent a moment. When she spoke again, her voice was quiet. "Maybe we should tell the truth."

"What do you mean?" In some ways, they were being honest. He'd broken up with her so he could pursue his career. He truly was a workaholic—he wouldn't have to pretend to play that part.

"We can tell them that you want biological children. I can't give them to you."

His heart cracked at her words. "Ainsley, no. That's not the reason."

"Are you sure?" she whispered.

"No," he said firmly. Taking a chance, he reached over and took her hand in his. "You know that's not why I left…before."

She turned to look out the window so he couldn't see her face, but didn't speak. A sense of urgency gripped him, desperation clawing at the edges of his thoughts. Did she really think he'd broken up with her because they couldn't have children together?

Had she spent the last five years believing she was somehow to blame for his actions?

He had to make it clear that wasn't the case. But what could he say to convince her he was telling the truth? That he'd left because the fault was within him, not with her?

"Ainsley, I told you the truth. I broke up with you because I needed to move to New York to pursue my career, and I knew you didn't want to leave your family here.

"Please believe me," he said. "The kid thing didn't matter to me. We could have always adopted, if that's what we both wanted." He was telling the truth. Part of him had been disappointed when she'd told him she was unable to have children. But he'd never felt compelled to become a father, never had that all-consuming desire to have children. Santiago had always thought that kids deserved to be born into a family that wanted them more than anything. Since he didn't want kids more than anything that way, he was happy remaining child-free.

"All right," she said finally, but it was clear from her tone she still had doubts. "It's fine. We can still use it as part of our story, if you want."

"No," he said, putting a little steel into his voice. "I'm not going to ask you to expose yourself to these people. They don't deserve your pain. Besides, it wasn't true then, and it isn't true now. We'll just stick with the original script." He searched for something else to say, hoping to lighten the mood. "You can say you hate my family, too."

She turned to look at him and he glimpsed the curiosity on her face before returning his gaze to the road. "I never met your parents," she said.

He huffed out a laugh. "Trust me. That was for a reason." He didn't enjoy spending time with his family. Gabriela was fine, but his mom and dad had spent so many years antagonizing each other they didn't know how else to behave. Even if he got them one-on-one, they spent the entire visit complaining about the other person so that there was no way to have a real conversation. For the sake of his own mental health, Santiago limited his contact with his parents to emails and the occasional phone call.

"It seems wrong that this is all your fault," she mused. "I mean it makes sense from my perspective that I would blame you for everything. But they're going to want to know why you're happy to end things. We need to come up with some issues that you have with me, so it seems realistic that you'd be willing to walk away as well. Otherwise, why wouldn't you want to fight for us?"

He considered her words as he took the next freeway exit and maneuvered the car onto the access road. What she said made sense—it would be a little suspicious if the impetus for the breakup was all one-sided. "Do you have any ideas?" he asked.

"What if we told them I had an affair?" she suggested. "I blamed you for working too much and being out of town all the time, so I cheated on you."

The idea of Ainsley with another man triggered a reflexive spurt of jealousy, but he quickly tamped it down. He had no claim on her, no right to be offended or hurt if she was with someone else. Her relationship status was a question he hadn't thought to ask earlier. Was that because he didn't want to know the answer?

"That's a good idea," he said. "Um, I probably should have asked you this before, but are you seeing anyone right now?" He held his breath, waiting for her to reply.

"No."

Santiago relaxed as some of the tension left his body. Her answer shouldn't have mattered to him, but it did. The small, selfish part of him didn't want to think about her with another man. No one was good enough for her—he could say that with authority. Even he had spent many an hour wondering what he'd done to deserve her affections. Her love was a gift, one he hadn't taken for granted. But in the end, he'd had to acknowledge she'd be better off without him.

"What about you? I know you're single now, but has there been anyone special since you moved to New York?"

Her question caught him off guard. He hadn't expected her to be curious about his own personal life, since she'd made it clear she was only helping him because he'd agreed to take her brother's case. Did she feel the same twinge of jealousy at the thought of another woman in his life? Or was she simply curious, wondering about his path since they'd parted ways?

"Ah, no," he said, deciding not to elaborate. He hadn't exactly been living the life of a monk, but he hadn't found anyone he really clicked with, either.

She didn't reply, and he couldn't see her expression so he didn't know what she was thinking. Hopefully, his single status would help convince her that he really had been telling the truth five years ago— he'd left to work on his career, not because he wanted to trade her in for a different model. He'd should have made that clear years ago, but he just hadn't been able to talk about his fears regarding commitment with her. At the time, it had seemed easier to use his career aspirations as the excuse to end their relationship.

They were silent the rest of the drive, which wasn't very long. In a matter of minutes, he turned off the two-lane country road onto a gravel drive. The car bounced along for about a hundred yards until the drive ended in a small paved parking lot. He pulled into a spot and turned off the engine, and together, they stared at the large log cabin situated about twenty yards away.

"Nice," Ainsley observed, turning her head to look at the smaller cabins nestled among the trees nearby. It was clear the large cabin was the main gathering center, and Santiago imagined the smaller ones were lodgings for the couples at the retreat.

The whole thing had a slick, polished feel to it. Flowerbeds lined the sidewalk to the main cabin, bursting with color. The grass was green and clipped, and the trees cast dappled shade on everything. Under any other circumstances, he would have enjoyed staying at a place like this.

"It seems cheating people pays well," he observed. If the grounds looked this nice, the interior must be amazing as well. The Woodses had an image to maintain, after all.

Santiago turned to look at Ainsley. "Last chance." He wasn't going to force her to stay and play the part of his wife, especially after her earlier tears. He had no intention of letting the Woodses get away with their fraudulent behavior, but he also wasn't willing to emotionally torture Ainsley to expose them as cheats and liars.

A glint of determination shone in her eyes. "I'm ready. Are you?"

He smiled, relieved to know she was on his team. "Let's do this."

Chapter 4

Ainsley took a deep breath, trying to calm the nerves jangling in her stomach. She'd never been much of an actress. Hopefully she could pull this off. Spencer hadn't been thrilled when she'd told him what she was doing, but then again, she hadn't been looking for his approval. She'd simply wanted to let him know what was going on, in case there was any trouble.

Santiago walked next to her as they moved up the path, side by side. The sunlight glinted off the emerald she wore on her left hand, the stone the same color as the trees around them. She still wasn't used to the feel of the band around her finger. But it was a gorgeous set, and a small, girlish part of her felt a little thrill every time she glanced down and caught sight of the jewelry.

Since when have I been distracted by shiny things? she mused silently, tearing her gaze away from the ring.

She jumped when Santiago took her hand. Without thinking, she pulled away. He slid her a glance. "We're splitting up, remember?" she whispered.

"I know," he replied in a low voice. "Nice job."

He held open the door to the main building, and she walked past him. The truth was, she hadn't been thinking of their facade when she'd pulled away. She'd simply reacted on instinct; it had been five years since he'd tried to hold her hand, and the men she'd dated after him hadn't been interested in public displays of affection. Ainsley simply wasn't used to casual physical contact.

But part of her wished she hadn't rejected his touch. Her skin tingled where they'd made contact. The sensation was a nice distraction from her nerves, and his gesture was a timely reminder that they were in this together.

Still, she probably shouldn't look to Santiago for reassurance. They *were* supposed to be splitting up. Her awkwardness and discomfort would help make them appear like a genuine couple in trouble. If she was too comfortable, too relaxed in his presence people would wonder why they were ending things.

She paused at the entrance, glancing around the foyer of the building. The air was cool and smelled of flowers, thanks to a large bouquet sitting on a table to the right. The walls were painted a soft green that paired nicely with hardwood floors the color of honey. She heard the soothing sounds of running water and spied a fountain just past the hospitality desk that was located straight ahead.

She felt the warmth of Santiago's body at her back, but he was careful not to touch her. *Good*, she thought, trying not to be disappointed. Her brain knew there couldn't be anything between them again, but that kiss in her office had convinced her body there was still hope. As a result, she felt conflicted, her baser wants at war with her logical self. This week would be an exhausting struggle, but she knew which side had to win.

"Do you see anyone here?" he said softly.

"No," she replied, glancing around as though an employee might jump out from behind the flowers. "Maybe we just sign in?"

They approached the tall desk together, their footsteps tapping on the floor and echoing slightly in the otherwise quiet room. Just as they reached the counter, a young man stepped forward from a room off to the left that they hadn't seen from the front door.

"Hello, and welcome to The Marriage Institute." He smiled politely, revealing straight, white teeth. "My name is Brett. You must be Mr. and Mrs. Rodriguez." It was the pseudonym Santiago had chosen for this retreat, not wanting anyone to make the connection between him and his sister Gabriela.

Ainsley frowned slightly, taken aback by this young man's familiarity. "How did you know that?"

He nodded in her direction. "You're the last ones to arrive for this week's retreat."

"Are we late?" Santiago asked. "I was told we should get here at five."

Brett chuckled. "Not to worry. Everything is fine. Please, let's get you checked in." He gestured to the tall counter and motioned for them to follow him over.

Ainsley let Santiago take care of the details. There was something about this young man that seemed off to her, though she couldn't quite put her finger on what, exactly, bothered her. He was pleasant and polite, and he looked like a model employee in his pressed khaki pants and light blue oxford shirt. Even his hair was on its best behavior, with none of the golden strands out of place. Why, then, did he make her uncomfortable?

"All right, Mr. and Mrs. Rodriguez. We're all set. Allow me to show you to your cabin."

They walked out of the main lodge, back onto the path. "Do you have any luggage?" Brett asked.

"Just two bags," Santiago replied.

"Let me help you with them."

Ainsley hung back, allowing Brett to carry her bag. She didn't want to get close to him, didn't want to risk touching him.

The path split close to the main building, with one

path branching off to the left. Brett led them down this walk, which took them deeper into the trees.

Ainsley looked around as they walked, trying to get a sense of the layout of the place. She knew from her online research there were five cabins arranged behind the main building, and she'd seen another small building on the map that wasn't identified. *Storage?* she'd wondered. *Or something else?*

Now that she was seeing the compound in person, she was surprised at how spread out everything was. The map had made it look like the cabins were close to each other, but she realized that wasn't the case at all. There were at least fifty yards between each cabin, and as they moved deeper into the trees, the main building seemed to recede into the distance.

"Here we are," Brett said cheerfully. He walked up the porch steps and unlocked the door, gesturing for them to precede him inside. Ainsley stepped onto the porch and cast a last look around before stepping inside—their cabin appeared to be the farthest away from the main building.

Brett placed her bag on the floor by the door. "Welcome to your home for the week," he said. "As you can see, there is a small kitchen area, which we've outfitted with a coffee maker and a teakettle. We've stocked the fridge with cream, but we ask that you enjoy your meals at the main house." He smiled at each of them in turn, as though this was a perfectly natural request.

"There are two bedrooms and two bathrooms,"

he continued, gesturing to the hallway off the main room. "One set on each side of the cabin. Each bedroom is large enough for two people. We understand you each might need your space during this time, but we encourage you to come together as often as possible to discuss your feelings and process the important work you'll be doing during your sessions."

Okay, this was getting a little too weird. Ainsley had never before had someone suggest how she should spend her time, and she didn't appreciate Brett's thoughts on the matter of her bed.

"Finally," he continued, "you'll find we have some amenities at the main cabin, such as an exercise room and a sauna. The main cabin is open from six in the morning to eleven at night every day, and we serve meals at eight thirty, noon and six. Follow the path from your cabin, and you'll have no trouble making your way back."

"What about the Woodses?" Santiago asked. "When will we meet them?"

Brett smiled, and Ainsley realized why she didn't like him: he was putting on an act. Everything about his behavior was fake, his bland pleasantness a front that gave no hint of real human emotion. He was like a Ken doll come to life, an automaton rather than an actual person.

"Alva and Brody will stop by your cabin after you've had a chance to settle in. They make it a point to greet every couple personally after they arrive."

"Wonderful," Ainsley murmured. She was ready

for this man to leave, so she and Santiago could talk in private.

Brett turned his smile on her, making her uncomfortable. "Thanks for your help," she said, hoping he would take his cue.

He did. "My pleasure. Please, don't hesitate to reach out if I can make your stay more pleasant. Just dial 9 from the phone, and you'll connect to the front desk."

"Thank you," Santiago said.

They were silent as Brett walked to the door and let himself out. Ainsley waited until she heard his footsteps fade on the gravel of the path before turning to Santiago.

He lifted a hand before she could speak, silently bidding her to remain quiet. As she watched, he took a small black device from his pocket and pressed a button. A green light appeared on top of the device, and Santiago began to walk around the cabin.

She followed him as he entered every room, holding the device in front of him as though it were some kind of divining rod. He led her back into the main room of the cabin and sat on the overstuffed cream sofa, then patted the cushion next to him.

Ainsley lowered herself onto the plush seat, watching as he turned the device off. "Did you just sweep the place for listening devices?" She was part astonished, part impressed. She'd never considered the possibility the place might be bugged.

Santiago nodded. "Yep. And I'll do it again after the Woodses leave, in case they turn them on later."

"Do you really think they spy on the couples here?"

He shrugged. "Who knows? Although I wouldn't be surprised. They're probably looking for any advantage to scam these people."

"I didn't like Brett," she said. "He's just too…" she trailed off, trying to articulate her thoughts.

"Brainwashed," Santiago supplied.

"Yes!" She nodded, glad he'd seen it, too. "That's exactly it."

"Yeah, he's definitely drunk the Kool-Aid," Santiago said. He shook his head. "I almost feel bad for the kid."

"Do you think the Woodses will have that same vibe?" Ainsley shuddered at the thought of having to spend the next week in this atmosphere. It was like the beginning of a horror movie, where everything was just a little bit skewed.

"I hope not," Santiago said. "Since they're the ones in charge, hopefully they're a little more natural." He glanced around the room. "Seems like a nice enough place to spend the week."

Ainsley nodded. "Yeah. If the circumstances were different, this would be a pretty little vacation spot."

The room was spacious, outfitted in shades of cream and forest green. The back wall and hallway were mostly windows, looking out on the trees beyond. She'd glimpsed the kitchenette when they'd walked in, spying cream counter tops and honey-blond cabinets.

"Which bedroom do you want?"

Their quick tour had revealed the bedrooms were arranged as mirror opposites, containing a queen-size bed, a chair and a simple wooden dresser. One had been decorated in shades of purple, the other in shades of blue.

"I'll take the purple one," she said.

She laughed as a look of relief crossed Santiago's face. "Not a fan?"

"It's not my favorite color," he admitted. "But if you wanted the blue room I'd deal."

"I'm not going to torture you," she said. She stood and walked over to pick up her bag. "I guess I'll unpack while we wait."

"Good idea," Santiago took his bag and followed her down the hall. They reached the end, and she turned right while he turned left.

Ainsley paused in the doorway to the bedroom and glanced back. "Santiago?"

He turned to face her. "Yeah?"

"I hope we bring these guys down." They hadn't even started the retreat yet, hadn't offered their bribes or been subject to the dubious therapy sessions. But she already disliked the place and had a feeling it was even worse than his sister had described.

He grinned, teeth flashing white in the shadows of the hallway. "We will."

* * *

The knock came shortly after six.

Ainsley had just finished brewing a cup of tea in the small kitchen. Santiago glanced at her, and she nodded.

Ready to meet the enemy.

He opened the door to find a middle-aged couple standing on the porch. "Welcome to The Marriage Institute. I'm Brody Woods, and this is my wife, Alva."

"Santiago Rodriguez," he replied, automatically sticking out his hand.

Brody had a firm handshake, strong but not painfully so. Alva offered him a smile and held up a brown paper bag. "May we come in for a moment?" she asked.

"Of course." Santiago stepped aside to let them past, though what he really wanted to do was drag them to a jail cell.

Easy does it, he reminded himself. As satisfying as it would be to unleash his anger on these two, he needed to keep the end goal in mind. Gather evidence, then bring them down.

They looked like a nice couple, a stereotypical middle-class pair. He wore khakis and a button-down shirt, his blond hair shot through with silver. She was a plump, matronly type, her short hair permed and teased to perfection. Her large glasses magnified her eyes, making her look a bit like an owl.

"We brought food," she said in a singsong announcement. She placed it on the small table in the kitchen area and smiled, looking pleased with herself. "It's not fancy, but we wanted to make sure you both had something to eat tonight. The kitchen in the main cabin doesn't open until tomorrow morning."

"Thank you." Ainsley spoke softly, and Santiago could tell by her tone that she was struggling to appear friendly. He couldn't blame her, and hopefully if the Woodses picked up on her negativity, they'd assume it was directed at him. After all, their marriage was in trouble, right?

Alva nodded. "Our pleasure. We're so glad you're here."

Santiago nearly snorted. Of course they were. As far as the Woodses were concerned, he and Ainsley were two more marks to swindle.

"I'm glad we could fit this into our schedule," he said. "And even happier you had room for us at the retreat."

Brody spread his arms out, and for a split second, Santiago was afraid the other man was going to try for a hug. "Our mission is to help couples in trouble. As licensed counselors, we've made it our life's work to teach other people how to effectively communicate and save their relationships." His tone was earnest; if Santiago hadn't known better, he might have believed the older man.

Alva stepped forward and placed what he supposed was meant to be a comforting hand on his arm. Santiago fought the urge to recoil from her touch.

"You've both taken the first step, which is often the most difficult." She glanced to Ainsley and back to him, clearly speaking to them both. "Your presence here means you're both committed to doing the hard work of repairing your relationship. We are so happy to help with that."

Ainsley merely nodded. Alva aimed a smile at her. "We're looking forward to getting to know you both over the next week. Remember, if you need anything, we're here to help."

"Thank you," Santiago said.

Brody tilted his head toward Ainsley. "We hope you enjoy your evening. The facilities at the main cabin are closed for the evening—we want everyone to wait to meet each other until our first session in the morning. Please get some rest, and we'll see you at breakfast."

"That sounds good," Santiago replied. "Let me walk you out." He stepped to the door and held it open. As the Woodses passed him, he shot Ainsley a look.

She nodded, understanding his silent signal.

Santiago closed the door behind him and indicated Alva and Brody should walk down the porch steps with him. While their backs were turned, he ran a finger over the surface of his own hidden camera, disguised as a coin he wore on a chain around his neck. "I was hoping to have a word in private?"

"Of course." Brody's tone was friendly, but he'd

dropped his voice to match Santiago's volume. "What's on your mind?"

Santiago stopped and lifted his hand to scratch the back of his head. "Here's the thing," he said. He made a point of glancing back at the cabin, as if he was worried Ainsley was spying on them. "This isn't going to work. I'm only here so that I can tell the divorce lawyer I tried everything. We have a pre-nup agreement that states we have to try counseling before we split or else she gets half of everything. Since we're both lawyers, it's not going to be easy to divorce. But I want out of this marriage."

The Woodses exchanged a look. "I see," Alva said carefully.

"Is there something you can do to help me?" he asked. "Maybe you can convince Grace that she'd be better off without me? If she initiates the divorce, I'll be able to argue down the amount of alimony she should get." It felt strange to use Ainsley's middle name, but he needed to get used to saying it around these people.

Brody nodded, his expression thoughtful. "You're not the first man to ask us this."

Santiago lifted his eyebrows, trying to look earnest. "That's why I came here. A friend of a friend said you guys work magic in these situations."

Alva and Brody exchanged a look. She nodded imperceptibly, and he turned to Santiago. "I think we can help you, if this is really what you want."

Santiago sighed as though relieved. "It is. What's it going to take?"

"We'll talk to your wife," Alva said. "We'll make sure she realizes she would be happier on her own. But to do that, we're going to have to paint you in an unflattering light. Are you going to be okay with that?"

Santiago nodded vigorously. "I don't care what you say about me. Just get me free."

"Funny you should use that word," Brody said. "I hope you can appreciate that when we take on a special project like this, it goes beyond the scope of the fees that you paid to attend the marriage retreat."

Santiago reached into his back pocket and pulled out an envelope. He passed it to Brody, who opened it and flipped through the bills.

"Four thousand now. Six thousand when she signs the divorce papers at the end of the week."

Brody passed the envelope to Alva, then smiled at him. "That's fair," he said.

"We can't offer any guarantees," Alva said firmly. "We will do our best, but for obvious reasons we make no promises."

"I understand," Santiago said.

"That means no refunds," Alva continued. She arched one brow, as though daring him to challenge her on this. "And we ask that you are discreet about our arrangement during the retreat."

"Of course." Santiago nodded. "I won't say a word. I don't want her suspecting anything."

"She won't," Brody said confidently. "Like I said before, you're not the only one we've helped. The spouses never know."

He smiled smugly, and Santiago fought the urge to punch the man in the nose. How many people had they hurt, all for the sake of a few dollars?

"Excellent," Santiago replied. "Thank you."

"Thank *you*, Mr. Rodriguez," Alva said. She tucked the envelope into her pocket with a smile. "I'm glad we'll be able to help you with your problem."

"Me, too," he said. "I'll see you in the morning." He waved goodbye and walked back to the cabin, his body shaking with anger. He swiped across the surface of his camera, turning it off again.

Ainsley took one look at his face when he walked in and stood up from where she'd been sitting on the sofa. "What happened?"

He shook his head. "They accepted the bribe."

She pressed her lips together, her expression disgusted. "Of course they did."

"They were so casual about it," he said, reliving the conversation in his mind. He felt strangely disconnected from the events, even though they had happened only a few minutes ago. "Like it was the kind of thing they do every day."

"They probably do," she pointed out.

"Who does that?" he asked, trying to wrap his brain around their casual, callous disregard for the welfare of others. He looked at her, hoping she had some insight as to what made these people tick.

Ainsley's eyes were full of warmth as she stared up at him. "I don't know." She stepped closer and placed her hand on his arm, almost in the same spot where Alva had touched him earlier. Her warmth burned away the hidden stain Alva had left behind, and he felt himself relax. "Try not to waste your time trying to understand them. It's not worth your emotional energy. All that matters is their actions, and they've proven they aren't trustworthy or decent people."

"I know, I just..." he trailed off, shaking his head. "I guess I'm trying to make sense of this. Don't get me wrong—I hate what they did to my sister, and to everyone else they hurt. I wish there had been enough evidence for the other people to press charges. I'm not trying to make excuses for them. I just want to know how two normal-looking people decided to go down this path. Did they wake up one day, look at each other and say, 'Let's start taking bribes!' Were they desperate for money? What do they tell themselves so they can sleep at night?"

Ainsley gave him a crooked smile, amusement dancing in her eyes.

"What?" he asked. "Why are you giving me that look?"

She shook her head. "Just remembering law school, and all those times in mock trial when you persuaded the jury to cut your client some slack.

You'd always weave a detailed story about their actions, their life, their motivations. You could make even the most hardened killer seem sympathetic when you were done."

"Hey now," he protested. "You know I'm very selective about my clients. I don't do image rehabilitation for true monsters."

"I'm not saying you do," she replied. "But you're very good at presenting the human side of people, of making juries think about why your clients make the choices they do. I don't think you try to make the truly guilty appear innocent. You just offer a nuanced perspective to ensure the jury doesn't make a knee-jerk decision without first accepting the humanity of your client."

He tilted his head to the side. "Are you saying that's a bad thing?"

"Not at all." She squeezed his arm and dropped her hand. "I admire that about you, the way you can see the good in people who, at first glance, don't seem to have any inside. But I think in this instance, your empathy is misplaced."

Santiago frowned. "What do you mean?"

Ainsley sighed softly. "When you're working, you're able to maintain a professional distance from your clients. It's just a job. But this is personal. The Woodses hurt your sister, and who knows how many others. This isn't just a case you can set aside at the end of the day. We're going to be around them all week, watching them work up close, all the while knowing they're lying and cheating and hurting people. It's going to be hard to do that, to bear witness to their behavior without trying to stop them. But we have to."

"I know," he said quietly. In truth, he'd thought he'd be able to handle it. But after spending only a few minutes around Brody and Alva, he knew Ainsley was right. It was going to take all his self-control to keep his anger in check during the week.

"Hey." Ainsley's voice was soft in the otherwise silent cabin. She touched his arm again, this time laying her hand flat against the side of his biceps. When he met her eyes, he saw her gaze was filled with understanding. "We're in this together, remember?"

Her words warmed him from the inside, making him feel less alone. If only that were really true! Sure, she was here with him now, helping him as he sought to expose the Woodses for the frauds they were. But that was as far as their partnership went. After the week was up, they'd go their separate ways, back to their individual lives with their own problems.

It was fine. It's what he'd wanted five years ago. Still wanted, come to that.

So why did the thought give him a twinge of regret?

He frowned, pushing aside his internal disquiet. He had one job this week: gather the evidence needed to tear down this sham of a marriage retreat and bring the Woodses to justice. His own emotional turmoil would have to wait.

Besides, once he got away from Ainsley, he would no longer feel that old familiar pull.

Right?

"We can do this," Ainsley said, misinterpreting the cause of his frown. "You and me. No time for second thoughts now."

He forced himself to smile. "I can't tell you how much I appreciate your help."

"Don't mention it," she replied. "I'll admit, I was skeptical at first. But now that I've met them and they've already taken your bribe, I know we're doing the right thing." She slid her arms around him, squeezing tightly in a fierce hug.

The movement caused her breasts to flatten against his chest. Santiago sucked in a breath as a zing of lust shot through him, igniting a fire of need in his belly. *Cool it*, he thought. It was clear Ainsley wasn't making a come-on; she was simply trying to offer him comfort. What kind of cad would he be if he responded to her innocent gesture with arousal?

After a few endless seconds, she pulled back, gazing up at him with a smile. It was the first truly unguarded look she'd given him since he'd stepped into her office earlier in the week, and the sight of it nearly took his breath away. This was the Ainsley he'd missed; full of life, a little mischievous, a lot passionate. He knew from experience that when she turned her focus on something or someone, she devoted herself entirely. It was a hell of a thing, to be on the receiving end of her attentions.

He cleared his throat, needing to shift his own mental focus before he let himself get carried away. "Are you hungry?"

She wrinkled her nose. "Kind of. But do you think we can trust the food they brought?"

"It's probably fine," he said. "I can't imagine they're in the business of poisoning their clients. Can't get money out of dead people, right?"

She laughed. "True. That reminds me—why don't you do another sweep of the place? Make sure they haven't turned anything on now that they paid us a visit."

"Good call." Santiago collected the detector from his room and walked around the cabin, double-checking their privacy. Once again, the place came up clear.

"Still nothing," he said, walking back into the kitchenette.

Ainsley nodded as she rummaged in the bag Alva had left behind. "Looks like sandwiches in here," she said, pulling out a few plastic cartons. "Along with some chips."

"Works for me," Santiago said. He was still too keyed up to eat, his emotions suppressing his hunger.

She placed everything on the table and sat in one of the chairs. He took the seat opposite hers and pulled one of the sandwiches in front of him. "In a twisted way, I suppose we're off to a good start," he remarked.

Ainsley took a bite and eyed him over the top of her sandwich. "Because they took the bribe?" she asked around her mouthful of food.

Santiago took his own bite and nodded. "It was so easy. Almost too easy." He frowned, seeing their conversation in a new light. He'd thought he was trapping them, but did the Woodses have something up their own sleeves?

"I wouldn't read too much into that," Ainsley said. "I'm sure they won't hesitate to throw you under the bus and tell me you bribed them if they think it will help them, but since I'm in on it, it doesn't matter."

"That's true," Santiago replied. "They probably think I'm just as compromised as they are."

"How are you going to get the money back, anyway?"

He shrugged. "I expect the judge who hears the case will order them to repay me, since I have them on tape taking the bribe."

"Fair enough." Ainsley shook her head and laughed. "You know, it's kind of nice feeling like the smartest one in the room."

Santiago nearly choked on his food. "Aren't you used to that already?"

"Hardly." Her tone was dry, the aural equivalent of rolling her eyes.

"Oh, come on," he insisted. "You were the smartest one in our class at law school. And no offense to your family, but I doubt any of your relatives are anywhere close to your level of intelligence."

"Flattery isn't necessary," she said, raising one eyebrow in a clear expression of skepticism. "I'm already here. No need to keep trying to convince me."

"It's not flattery, it's the truth," he shot back. "You're the smartest person I know."

She shifted in her chair and he knew she was uncomfortable. She'd always had a hard time accepting praise, a habit he'd never understood. When they'd been together, he'd tried to help her see just how amazing she was. He was willing to bet that once they'd separated, she'd had no one in her life to hold up a mirror so she would recognize her own accomplishments.

The thought made him sad. Ainsley was special, but she'd always minimized her own gifts, preferring the shadows to the spotlight.

It's not your problem, he reminded himself. A part of him would always care for Ainsley—he was smart enough not to deny or fight it. But he couldn't be there for her, not in the way a true partner was. And if he let himself get too close, if he started to forget why he'd left her in the first place, he'd only hurt them both in the end.

She cleared her throat. "Maybe I can get them one-on-one tomorrow morning after breakfast," she said. "Offer them my bribe and see what happens."

"That sounds like a plan." Santiago nodded, glad

the conversation was moving on. Best to focus on why they were here and ignore any other distractions.

It was the only way he was going to get through this.

Chapter 5

"Welcome to breakfast." The young woman smiled at them, nodding first at Santiago, then at Ainsley, the following morning. "If you'll please follow me, I'll show you to your table. This is where you both will eat your meals for the duration of your stay with us."

Interesting, Ainsley thought as they followed the staffer into a dining room off the main lobby. It seemed the Woodses didn't want the couples at the marriage retreat speaking to each other outside of any group sessions. Was that because they didn't want people comparing notes? It was definitely easier to manipulate people if you isolated them. Given the fact the Woodses had insisted they stay in their cabins last night, and were now assigning them all to separate tables, it seemed they were starting the process early.

The dark-haired woman stopped at a two-top and flashed that Stepford smile once more. "Here you are."

"Thank you," Santiago said quietly. They sat across from each other, and Ainsley glanced around the room.

There were nine other tables, all of them set for only two people. Six couples were here already, sipping coffee or eating scrambled eggs. There was a quiet hum of conversation in the air, but she couldn't make out any individual words.

The room itself matched the subtle, classy decor of their cabin and the lobby they'd seen yesterday. The sound of a fountain tinkled through the room, the soothing noise providing additional privacy for speech.

Not that it mattered. The tables were set far apart, islands scattered throughout the room. The better to discourage casual socialization, she supposed.

Santiago caught her eye. "Interesting setup," he said softly.

She nodded. "For a couple who claims to be all about encouraging communication, it sure doesn't seem that way."

A twentyish-looking man appeared at their table, looking like a catalog model. "Coffee?" he asked brightly.

Santiago and Ainsley both nodded, and he filled their cups. "I'll tell the kitchen you're here. The food will be out momentarily."

"We don't get to order from a menu?" Ainsley asked.

The waiter shook his head. "No, ma'am. The Woodses have carefully curated the menu for this retreat, choosing foods specially designed to help you focus and cleanse your body. Since neither of you indicated any food allergies in your application paperwork, you're able to partake of every meal."

"Wonderful," Ainsley said dryly.

The young man didn't appear to pick up on her sarcasm. His smile brightened, an event Ainsley hadn't thought possible. "I think you'll find the food to be delicious."

He disappeared, and Ainsley shot Santiago a look. "The brainwashing seems to have already begun."

A spark of amusement flared in his dark eyes, making her stomach do a little flip. "Gotta start early," he said.

His voice was deep and soft. Ainsley took a deep breath, determined to ignore the physical reaction. It was a reflex, nothing more.

She reached for the coffee and took a fortifying sip. Truth be told, she hadn't slept well last night, and not just because of the unfamiliar surroundings.

Being around Santiago was unsettling. Hugging him last night had been a mistake. The last thing she needed was a visceral reminder of the way their bodies fit together. The kiss in her office had thrown her for a loop, but she'd pushed aside the emotions that had stirred up. But that hug? Feeling her body press against his, her breasts flattening against the solid plane of his chest, the way his arms had circled round her...that was harder to ignore.

And then there was the way he'd looked at her last night, when he'd told her she was the smartest person he knew. The statement had nearly made her cry, though she shouldn't have been surprised. Santiago had always been supportive of her endeavors. He wasn't the type of man who had to put others down in order to feel superior, and he'd never been threatened by her intelligence. He was one of the only men she knew who seemed to enjoy her brains, rather than merely tolerate them.

Each event, taken on its own, would be tolerable. But all together? It was adding up to be trouble.

Her thoughts were interrupted by the waiter, who slid a plate in front of her. She eyed the food, expecting something unusual after that nonsense about "focus and cleansing" the waiter had spouted earlier. But everything looked normal: eggs, whole-grain toast and a side of fresh fruit. A sliced avocado sat off to the side, along with a small pot of jelly.

"This looks...decent." She poked at the eggs with her fork and reached for the pepper.

"Tastes okay, too," Santiago said around a mouthful.

Ainsley glanced up, surprised he was already chowing down. "You trust them?"

He lifted one shoulder in a shrug. "Like I said last night, it's not in their best interest to poison us."

"That's true." She forked up a bite of eggs, pleased to find they were fluffy. Despite their flaws, it seemed the Woodses hired decent chefs.

Movement from the side of the room caught her eye, and she turned to see the couple was here.

Brody and Alva made their way to a small platform at the front of the room, smiling and nodding to people as they moved through the room. The remaining couples had filed in while she and Santiago hadn't been looking, and now it seemed they were all present and accounted for.

"Welcome, welcome," Brody said, spreading his arms wide, a smile on his face. "We're so glad you're here for our marriage retreat."

Standing at his side, Alva beamed up at him, the very picture of wifely devotion.

Ainsley refrained from rolling her eyes. Barely.

"Alva and I have been married for forty years," Brody continued. He looked down at his wife with an affectionate smile. "I think we've learned a thing or two, wouldn't you say, dear?"

The older woman giggled, the sound like nails on a chalkboard to Ainsley's ears. "We do have degrees in counseling as well, dear."

Brody smiled indulgently at his wife. "We are so excited to have you all join us. The fact that you're here means you've taken the first, most difficult step.

And it also shows that, despite your troubles, you each still value your marriage."

He paused to let that sink in. Ainsley saw several people nod, and noticed a few looks of surprise throughout the room, as though Brody's words had made these people realize something they hadn't considered before.

Her heart squeezed in empathy. Much as she hated to agree with him, Brody was right. These people were here because they were trying to get their relationships back on track. Or most of them were, at least. The fact that Brody and Alva were all too happy to cheat and lie and take advantage of their vulnerabilities made her blood boil.

"Now, this isn't going to be easy," Alva said. "We have a lot of work to do, and we're going to ask a lot of you. You're going to have to open your hearts and minds, and you're going to have to be vulnerable to each other. We're going to work to rebuild trust in your marriages, something that may have been lacking in the recent past."

There were a few rueful chuckles throughout the room. Alva nodded, apparently encouraged. "We can't promise results," she continued. "But Brody and I are proud of our track record. Over the last decade that we've been doing this retreat, 95 percent of the couples who attend go on to have stronger marriages after their time with us."

A few gasps of surprise punctuated this announcement. Ainsley kept her expression neutral, but inside, her BS detector was blaring. That seemed like an awfully inflated number, but with no way to verify the data, the Woodses could make whatever claims they wanted.

"We're going to be with you every step of the way," Brody chimed in. "We aren't asking you to do anything we haven't done. And we're going to be sharing with you, as well. We believe that experience is the best teacher. But we don't want you to have to experience all the trials and tribulations we've gone through. So we're going to take the lessons we've learned and share them with you."

"In all their embarrassing detail," Alva said.

Brody chuckled, along with the other couples in the room. As Ainsley scanned the faces in the room, she realized they were buying this spiel hook, line and sinker.

She glanced at Santiago, who was also smiling. If she hadn't known better, she would think he was swallowing this drivel as well.

His reaction made her realize she, too, had a part to play. So she pushed her true feelings aside and tried to act like she was happy to be here.

"If there's one thing I've learned," Brody said. "It's that pride will get you into a lot of trouble. I hope one of the things you'll all learn during the retreat is how to put your own selfish pride aside and focus on the good of your partner and your relationship. If you can learn that lesson, you'll be ready to face whatever life throws at you."

"But it won't be easy," Alva cautioned the room. "That's why we have so many sessions during this retreat. You'll each experience two individual counseling sessions per day, along with two couple's sessions. We also have one group session and one seminar every day."

Ainsley felt her eyebrows lift, and judging from the other expressions in the room, she wasn't the only one surprised by this schedule.

Alva held up a hand, anticipating objections. "I know that sounds like a lot. It is." She glanced up at Brody with a smile. "You've all made a significant financial investment to be here. Now we're asking you to match that with your time and effort. If you truly commit to the experience and put in the work, you will reap the rewards."

"She's right." Brody stepped forward, his avuncular demeanor making it seem like he was about to impart a nugget of wisdom. "That means put away your distractions—no phones, no work. I'm sure you've already noticed there are no televisions in your cabins."

"It's important you set aside the routines of your daily life in order to truly focus on healing the damages in your marriage," Alva added. "Only by breaking free of the chains of past habits and patterns can you truly move forward together."

Ainsley had to admit, they talked a good game. And some of what they said actually made sense. She knew from her own experience that she'd had to let

go of some of her habits after Santiago had left—
going to the same stores, the same restaurants had
been too hard, a painful reminder that what they'd
once done together she was now doing alone. So
she'd started trying new things, building a new set
of memories that didn't contain Santiago. It had been
difficult, but she'd done it. Moving back to Mustang
Valley after law school had helped with that, as he'd
never lived there. It only stood to reason that couples
in trouble would have to learn new ways of relat-
ing to each other, since their existing strategies had
brought them here in the first place.

"Your server will bring your personal schedules
to your tables shortly," Brody said. "Take a few moments to look them over, and we will see you soon
for your first session. All of you will be there, and
we will assign the smaller groups at that time."

With that, the pair stepped down from the stage
and began to make their way out of the room. Ainsley looked at Santiago. "I guess it's time for me to
offer my bribe," she said quietly.

He nodded. "Act like you're looking for the bathroom," he suggested.

"Good idea." She got to her feet and made a
show of looking around the room. Fortunately for
her, there wasn't a clearly marked sign identifying
the facilities, so it didn't look too odd that she was
wandering around.

Ainsley made sure she gave them a minute or
two to leave the room, so she didn't appear to be

chasing after them. She slipped out of the room and caught sight of their backs as they reached the end of the hallway.

Picking up the pace, she raced after them. As she ran, she ran a finger over the front of her necklace to activate the camera. "Excuse me!" she called out.

Brody turned, followed by Alva. "Yes?" Brody asked. "Did you need something?"

She came to a stop in front of them, panting slightly. "Yes," she said. "I was hoping to have a private word?"

Impatience flitted across Alva's face, so she quickly added, "I don't need much of your time."

The couple exchanged a cryptic look. "Of course," Brody said, his tone friendly. "What can we do for you? It's Grace Rodriguez, right?"

Ainsley nodded and stepped closer, dropping her voice. "It's my husband, Santiago," she said. "I have to get out of this marriage."

Alva's brows drew together, her expression one of maternal concern. "Oh my dear," she said. "What makes you say that?"

Ainsley glanced around, as though worried someone would overhear. "He's cheating on me," she nearly whispered. "Has been for years. I have proof, but he doesn't know that. I agreed to this retreat because he thinks he can use these sessions as an excuse to shortchange me on the alimony."

"I'm so sorry." Brody looked genuinely sympathetic.

"How can we help?" Alva asked.

"I need him to admit to his infidelity," Ainsley said. "If he confesses in one of the counseling sessions, then according to the terms of our prenup, I'll get everything."

Alva nodded gravely. "I see. Well," she trailed off, shaking her head. "We're sympathetic to your situation of course, but I'm sure you can appreciate that what happens in the individual counseling sessions must remain private. This is a safe space, and if people don't trust that what they say will be held in confidence, then they won't participate fully. It undermines our mission to bring people together."

Ainsley locked eyes with the older woman. "I understand," she said. "But I only want to know what Santiago says, not what anyone else talks about. And I'm willing to pay for the information." She slipped her hand into the back pocket of her pants and withdrew an envelope.

Alva and Brody exchanged another look, this one assessing. For a moment, Ainsley thought they were going to refuse her bribe. But then Brody extended his hand and took the envelope.

He handed it to Alva, who opened it and flipped through the bills inside. The older woman glanced up, the look on her face making it clear she wasn't impressed with the offer.

"Half now, half after you tell me what he says," Ainsley said, injecting a defensive note into her voice. "Do we have a deal?"

Brody looked at Alva, who gave a subtle nod. "Yes, Mrs. Rodriguez," he said, sticking his hand out to shake hers. "It would seem that we do."

"Excellent." Ainsley smiled. "Thank you for your help."

"Normally, we don't operate like this," Alva said. "But in cases of infidelity…"

"I understand," Ainsley said, offering the absolution the other woman seemed to be asking for. "I wouldn't have asked, but after what he's done, I'll never trust him again."

"There are some things that can't be fixed," Brody said seriously.

"I trust you'll remain discreet?" Alva asked. She seemed a little anxious, but there was a calculating glint in her eyes that made Ainsley think this was all just an act designed to make it look like they'd never taken a bribe before.

"Of course," Ainsley replied. "If Santiago's lawyer were to find out I paid to get this information, it would only hurt my case during the divorce."

Alva nodded, apparently satisfied by her response. "All right. We'll do what we can for you. Mind you, we can't force him to admit to anything. We can only encourage total honesty."

"I'll take any help you can give me," Ainsley said, trying to sound relieved.

"I think we'll be able to get you what you need," Brody said. He reached out to give her shoulder a pat, and Ainsley steeled herself not to flinch away from the contact. "Just relax and try to enjoy your time here. Even though your marriage is over, you might still find the seminars useful."

"That's true," she forced herself to say. "Maybe I can learn how not to make the same mistakes twice."

Brody smiled, a teacher pleased with his pupil's response. "Exactly." He dropped his hand, making Ainsley sigh internally with relief. "We'll see you at the first seminar," he said.

Ainsley nodded. "Looking forward to it," she replied.

The Woodses began walking away, and Ainsley turned and started back down the hallway that led into the dining room. After a few steps, she drew up short.

Brett was standing in the doorway to the dining room, that perma-smile fixed on his face. It was clear he'd been watching them, and a shiver ran down Ainsley's spine at the knowledge he'd been spying.

"Did you get the help you needed?" His voice was perfectly pleasant, his demeanor calm. But just as before, Ainsley's skin crawled at his proximity.

"Yes, thank you," she said.

He stepped to the side, his hand out to indicate she should precede him into the dining room. "May I escort you back to your table?"

"No, thanks," she replied quickly. "I can find it just fine on my own."

He nodded as she slipped past him, fighting the urge to contort her body to get as far away from him as possible. This time, she felt his eyes on her back as she headed toward Santiago.

She took her seat across from him, and he nodded at her. He lifted his coffee cup and held it in front of his mouth while he spoke. "You appear to have a shadow," he said softly.

Ainsley tried not to shudder. "I know."

"It's not just you," he added. "I've noticed that one of the employees follows anyone who has gotten up from the table. They stay at a distance, but it's clear they're watching where people are going."

"Making sure we don't talk to each other?" she wondered aloud. "Or keeping people from snooping?"

"Maybe a bit of both," he said. "Everything go okay?"

"Yep," she said shortly. "They took the bait. Now we just wait and see how this plays out."

Santiago nodded. "Good work." The note of approval in his voice made her want to preen, but she pushed down the inconvenient reaction. She didn't need his appreciation, damn it.

"It didn't take much effort on my part," she said. "I told them you'd been unfaithful, and they went with it." It was the story they'd agreed upon last night, one that would make it easy for them to track how the Woodses behaved. If they encouraged Santiago to confess his marital sins, they'd know her bribe had worked. If they tried to convince Ainsley she was better off on her own, they'd know Santiago's bribe held sway. Either way, they both had the Woodses on camera accepting bribes to skew the results of the marriage retreat.

It was the start of a rock-solid case. If only they could end things now and go back to their normal lives...

"Come on," Santiago suggested. He got to his feet, throwing his napkin on the table. "The first session starts in five minutes. We should head to the room."

"Sounds good." Ainsley rose as well and moved to stand by him. Together, they set off for the entrance, where one of the ever-present smiling employees stood to direct them to their next stop.

She stole a glance across the room as they left, back in the direction of where she'd pursued the Woodses. Brett still stood in the doorway, his eyes fixed on her. He noticed her look and nodded, his smile slipping a bit.

Ainsley swallowed, bile rising up the back of her throat. Something was going on behind the scenes here, she just knew it.

But did she really want to find out what it was?

He was going to go insane.

After two days at the marriage retreat, Santiago had just about reached his limits. He didn't think he could sit through one more group discussion, participate in another self-reflection, or handle an additional couple's therapy session.

It was all so...slick. So carefully crafted to manipulate the thoughts and feelings of the "chosen victim," as he'd taken to thinking about it. By now, it was clear the Woodses had picked his side and were actively working to wear down Ainsley so she would agree to an easy divorce. It was enough to turn his stomach, and the only thing that kept him going was the knowledge that Ainsley was here with him, and that she knew the truth.

She sat across from him now as they ate lunch together. He stole glances at her face between bites and wondered how anyone who had vowed to love, honor and respect someone could have their heart turned so drastically. He and Ainsley had never married, but he had loved her and he still cared deeply for her. He couldn't imagine getting to a point in their relationship where he would pay people to deliberately hurt her.

But that seemed to be what half the people in this room had done. Unless he missed his guess, most of the couples in the room had at least one person who had paid to sway the outcome of this retreat. He knew in his own group sessions, the counselor had focused on tips and tricks to manage the divorce process, everything from hiding assets to choosing an attorney. And wouldn't you know it, they just so happened to have a list of lawyers they could recommend if anyone was interested. He hadn't recognized any of the names on the list, but he'd definitely pass the info along to the police later. The whole thing made Santiago wonder just how big this racket really was—

were the bribes simply limited to the Woodses, or was there a network of people ready and waiting to profit off the misery of others?

Ainsley's experience had been quite the opposite, as though she was in a totally different retreat. She'd told him that members of her group were being counseled to move on, to maintain their dignity and let go without a fight. Based on what she'd told him, her group sessions had encouraged people to look inward, to blame themselves for the problems in their marriages. As he glanced at the faces around the room, he could tell based on the pinched, anxious expressions that the message seemed to be taking hold.

It was enough to make him want to end things now, to stop this charade and tell the Woodses he and Ainsley had them on camera accepting bribes. But that wasn't quite enough. They had to collect evidence proving the bribes had made a difference in how he and Ainsley were being treated, in the things that were said to them. Only then would he have the strongest case against them. Anything less, and there was a very real risk that the Woodses would be able to argue their way out of the lawsuit he planned to file as soon as this retreat was over.

"Are you okay?"

Ainsley's voice broke into his thoughts, and he looked up to find her watching him, concern shining in her eyes.

Santiago nodded. "Just thinking."

The corner of her mouth lifted in a wry smile. "Try not to," she advised. "You'll just get angry."

"How are you holding up?" he asked. "You're the one getting the short end of the stick here. At least in my sessions, the counselors are validating everything I say. I know it's fake, but it's got to be exhausting to be told you're in the wrong all the time."

She shrugged and dropped her eyes to her plate. "It's not fun," she said. "But I know not to take it personally. I'm worried for the people who actually believe what we're being told."

"No kidding." That's what kept him up at night; the innocent people in this situation who, through no fault of their own, were being manipulated into thinking they'd done something wrong.

"Five more days, right?" she said softly. "We can get through five more days."

Santiago nodded, knowing they had no other choice. "Eyes on the prize," he muttered.

Chapter 6

Three days later...

The thought kept circling around Ainsley's mind, a mantra she was silently chanting to herself to get through the current group counseling session. It was unbelievable, the way the other members in her "circle" were being told to let go and move on with their lives, or to forgive and forget, even though their spouses had been treating them badly for months, or even years.

"...so you see, Jenny," continued Alexa, one of the counselors Ainsley was quickly growing to hate, "while it's tempting to blame your husband for his infidelity, it's important to examine your emotional and sexual availability over the last several months. Have you been a true partner to him, or have you let the demands of your life intrude in your marriage?"

Jenny, a thirtysomething woman with limp blond hair and a long face, nodded. Her lower lip trembled as she stared up at Alexa, her eyes shiny with unshed tears.

"I know I've changed a lot since the baby came," Jenny said, her voice thick with emotion. "I went into survival mode right after the birth, and I was too exhausted to do anything more than take care of little George. I guess I just fell into the habit of focusing solely on him, since he was the most vocal about needing my attention."

Ainsley very nearly snorted in disgust. What kind of man cheated on his wife while she was taking care of their newborn son? What kind of narcissistic psychopath broke his marriage vows because his wife wasn't stroking his ego (or other bits) while recovering from childbirth?

Alexa nodded sagely, her expression patient. "That's exactly right," she said, her voice pitched low in a soothing cadence. "Your marriage existed before your son came along. You need to nurture the connection with your husband so he doesn't feel shut out of the new family dynamic."

"I'm, uh, still recovering from the birth." Jenny looked down at her lap and blushed. "I know it's been nine months, but there was a lot of stitching involved, and my doctor told me the kind of repairs I had will affect…things."

Alexa nodded again, like she understood exactly was Jenny was going through. In reality, the woman didn't have children—she'd said as much when she'd introduced herself at the beginning of the week.

"I know having a baby can be a physically traumatic experience," the counselor said. "But you've got to try to rekindle the flame for your husband."

"Even if it hurts?" Jenny's voice was impossibly small and Ainsley's heart broke for her. Her husband was even worse than she'd initially thought.

Alexa smiled brightly. "I'm sure the pain is partly in your mind. Besides, there are things you can do to help. Have you seen a therapist?"

Ainsley bit her lip to keep from screaming. The woman was clearly exhausted from the demands of caring for her baby, in addition to healing from what sounded like a difficult birth. She needed to ditch the man-child—in her case, she'd be better off alone than tied to a guy who pressured her for sex despite her pain, and cheated on her when she didn't fulfill all his needs.

"I don't know where to start with that," Jenny said.

"That's why we're here," Alexa replied. "You're already starting the process. At the end of the week, I can give you some recommendations so you can continue this important work of self-improvement for your husband and marriage."

Ainsley glanced around, wondering if anyone else thought Alexa was way out of line with the advice she gave to Jenny. But all she saw was a circle of nodding heads, everyone apparently on board with this casual display of cruelty toward a new mother.

"Well, we seem to be out of time at the moment. We'll take a break and pick things up again tomorrow. In the meantime, I want you all to reflect on the ways your behavior has contributed to the troubles in your marriage. Have you been emotionally and sexually unavailable, like Jenny? Or have you put your work above your partner?" She glanced around the room, smiling at everyone in turn. "Tomorrow, we'll start digging deeper into these common mistakes and learn about ways to make amends."

Ainsley grabbed her clutch and got to her feet, positioning herself so she was close to Jenny. As they filed out of the room, she gently touched the other woman's elbow.

Jenny looked back, startled. Ainsley offered her a small smile. "Do you have a minute to chat?"

"Okay." Jenny nodded, but she looked uncertain.

Ainsley led her into a small alcove off the hall, near a ficus tree standing in a nut-brown pot.

"I'm worried about you," Ainsley said softly.

Jenny's eyes widened. "Me? Why?"

Ainsley tilted her head to the side. "You're taking care of a new baby, probably on your own, am I right?"

Jenny looked down. "My husband works hard at

his job. He deserves a break when he gets home at the end of the day."

Anger bubbled through Ainsley's veins, making her feel hot. Those sounded like her husband's words coming out of her mouth. "And what about you? Don't you deserve a break?"

Jenny blinked, as though she hadn't thought about it that way.

"You're still healing from the birth," Ainsley continued. "He should not be pressuring you for sex, especially when he knows it causes you pain."

"I think I just need to relax," Jenny started.

Ainsley held up a hand. "I'm not a doctor. But do you have one you can trust? Maybe something didn't heal properly? It's worth getting checked out, for your own sake."

Jenny nodded, and Ainsley saw a light come into her eyes. "I think you're right." She studied Ainsley for a few seconds. "You seem to know a lot about this. Do you have kids?"

Ainsley shook her head, ignoring the prick of pain in her heart. "No." She debated telling Jenny the truth—that she couldn't have children, wasn't even sure if she wanted them, in fact—but decided against it.

"I have several close friends with kids, and my half sister just had one," she said instead. "So I've heard a lot about the delivery and recovery process."

"It's been really hard," Jenny said. She sounded almost confessional, as though she'd kept her doubts and struggles to herself for so long, she wasn't sure she should be talking about them now.

"I've heard," Ainsley said. And Jenny's situation was apparently made even more difficult thanks to her cad of a husband.

"He shouldn't be cheating on you," Ainsley said, feeling bolder now that they'd been talking on their own. "You don't deserve that."

Jenny looked down again, but not before Ainsley caught the sheen of tears in her eyes. "You don't think it's my fault?"

"Not at all," Ainsley conformed. "You shouldn't have to put up with that. If I were you, I'd leave him." She lowered her voice. "My husband is cheating on me, too. I know what it's like. But trust me, there's someone better out there for you, someone who won't sleep with other women and then try to blame you for his actions."

"I don't know," Jenny said sadly. "Steve says my body isn't what it used to be. He's right—I still haven't lost all of the baby weight."

Screw him! Ainsley screamed in her head. This guy had really done a number on Jenny's sense of self-worth. It was going to take more than one pep talk to help Jenny feel better about herself. But Ainsley had to try.

"Any true man would be lucky to have you," she said.

Jenny glanced up, a shy smile forming at the corners of her mouth. "Do you really think that?"

Ainsley nodded. "I wouldn't have said it otherwise."

"Maybe you're right," Jenny said, sounding tentative. "Maybe I—"

"Babe? Jenny, what are you doing back here?"

As soon as the male voice interrupted their conversation, Jenny retreated back into her shell. She seemed to grow smaller before Ainsley's eyes as her shoulders drew up and her head lowered.

"Hi, honey," she said. "I was just taking to one of the women from my group."

A man walked up and put a possessive hand on Jenny's arm. Even if Ainsley didn't know what he'd said and done to his wife, she would have disliked him on sight. He was a few inches taller than she was, with an arrogant air about him. His blond hair was combed to the side and shiny with gel. He sported khaki pants and a tucked-in polo shirt, the business casual uniform of corporate drones the world over. But it was his eyes that she found so repulsive— small, blue and mean.

He gave Ainsley the once-over, clearly suspicious. "Oh yeah? You know we're not supposed to talk to others outside of sessions." He tugged on Jenny's arm. "Come on. We don't want to be late for lunch."

Jenny gave Ainsley an apologetic glance before turning away. "Okay, Steve."

Steve released Jenny's arm and hung back while his wife walked away. He glared at Ainsley.

"What the hell do you think you're doing?" His voice was low and full of malice.

Ainsley bit her lip, stifling a knee-jerk reply. As satisfying as it would be to bring this man down to size, he was liable to take his anger out on Jenny. The other woman hadn't said there was any physical abuse going on, but as Ainsley took note of Steve's red face and clenched hands, she didn't trust that he wouldn't start beating his wife for talking out of turn.

"We were just chatting," Ainsley said. "We have some things in common. Jenny looked like she could use a friend."

Steve relaxed a bit, though he didn't quite seem to believe her. "She's fine," he said shortly. "She doesn't need any friends. She's got enough already."

"Why don't you let her decide that for herself?"

Steve took a small step forward. Ainsley stood her ground, refusing to be bullied. "Stay away from my wife," he said quietly.

Any other time, Ainsley would have pushed forward, ignoring this man's blatant intimidation tactics and doing what she wanted. But she just couldn't bring herself to make things harder for Jenny. The other woman had enough trouble as it was—the last thing Ainsley wanted was to add to the new mom's difficulties.

"I won't talk to her," Ainsley said, hating the words even though she knew they were necessary. It wasn't in her nature to back down from a bully, but she had to do what was best for Jenny.

"But," she added, "if Jenny speaks to me, I'm not going to ignore her."

"She won't," Steve said shortly. "She knows better than to do that."

He gave her one final glare and turned on his heel, walking quickly to catch up with his wife.

Ainsley watched them go, wincing in sympathy as she saw Steve's tight grip on the back of Jenny's arm. That was a man with control issues, and likely anger management problems as well. Unless she missed her guess, he'd very likely bribed the Woodses to help gaslight Jenny so she wouldn't leave him.

But why? Why hang on to a marriage he himself was disrespecting? Was it just for the image? Or something more?

Whatever his motivation, Ainsley hoped that when she and Santiago brought down the Woodses, this guy got what was coming to him as well.

Santiago shut the door of the cabin with a sigh and leaned back against the cool, wooden surface. He was physically exhausted, which made no sense at all. He'd spent most of his time over the past few days sitting—in group counseling sessions, in couple's therapy sessions, in one-on-one sessions. So. Much. Talking.

His body was stiff from disuse, his muscles achy with a need to move. If only he could muster the energy!

On some level, he'd known this would be an emotionally challenging week. What he hadn't predicted was the effort required to control his reactions, to sell his performance as a dissatisfied husband looking for a way out. No amount of time spent at the gym could provide that kind of conditioning.

He felt a touch on his arm and looked down to find Ainsley watching him, her brows drawn together in a slight frown. "Talk to me," she said. "I'm worried about you."

The corner of his mouth twitched. "I'm okay." Her concern warmed him from the inside, restoring some of his equilibrium. Her presence anchored him in reality, helping him shrug off the facade he wore all day during the retreat. He'd quickly come to look forward to their evenings in the cabin, the time they spent alone together giving him a chance to recharge and prepare for the next day of lies.

Their evenings had already fallen into a pattern, one that seemed to suit them both. They retired to the cabin after dinner and both changed into casual clothes. Ainsley made herself a cup of decaf coffee while he sipped on tea. Then they sat on the sofa and talked. Mostly about the events of the day, but other things, too. Like her brother's case. The interviews he'd managed to conduct before the retreat. What she thought might be going on, who could have sent that first, shocking email about her brother's parentage.

Occasionally, they would flirt with something more personal. But they usually skated around those topics, as if by silent mutual agreement. This week was already complicated enough. No need to make things more difficult.

The way she was watching him now, Santiago feared she was about to break their unspoken understanding. So he pushed off the door and headed for the kitchenette. "Just a long day," he said over his shoulder. "Want me to start your coffee?"

"That'd be great, thanks," she replied. "I'm going to go change."

"Take your time," Santiago said. The longer she was in the bedroom, the more time he'd have to regain his composure. It would be so, so easy to really open up and talk to Ainsley. But he couldn't let himself get emotionally involved with her again. It wouldn't be fair to either one of them.

He grabbed the small carafe and filled it with water from the tap, then poured it into the coffee maker. Once he got the coffee brewing, he started gathering the things for his tea. After a few minutes, he heard the soft sounds of Ainsley's slippered feet on the wood floor and knew she'd returned.

"So how was your day?" she asked around a yawn. "Learn anything new?"

Santiago turned around and leaned against the counter, crossing his arms over his chest. "Not really," he said. "Just more confirmation that some people are total monsters."

"Tell me about it," she said. She shook her head as she dropped into one of the chairs at the small table. "There's this woman in my group—her name is

Jenny. She opened up today during our group counseling session." She launched into the story of this
poor woman and her emotionally abusive husband.
Santiago felt his heart break for Jenny, and wished
there was something he could do to help her and her
son. Having grown up in a house with two parents
who hated each other, he knew firsthand the difficult childhood that was surely in store for the baby.

"I tried to talk to her after the session, but her husband interrupted us," Ainsley continued. "He was a
real jerk about it, too. Makes me wonder how much
worse he is behind closed doors, when he's not worried about making an impression on other people."

Santiago frowned. "What's his name again?"

"Steve." Her disdain practically dripped from the
word.

A tingle of worry shot down Santiago's spine. "I
know him from my sessions. He's a total ass."

"Yeah, I figured that out pretty quickly."

The coffee maker gurgled, signaling its completion. Santiago poured Ainsley a cup and placed a tea
bag in his own mug of steaming water. He carried
both to the table and took the chair opposite her. "No,
I mean he's got a temper."

Ainsley's eyes flashed with anger. "Is he hitting
her? She didn't mention physical abuse, but after
what I saw today, I wouldn't put it past him."

Santiago shook his head. "He hasn't mentioned
that, and I doubt he'd admit it. It's one thing to say
you're cheating on your wife because she's not in-

terested in sex anymore. It's quite another to confess to beating her."

Ainsley sipped her coffee with a frown. "I suppose you're right." She was silent a moment, then leaned forward. "I'm convinced he bribed the Woodses as well. Is there anything we can do to bring him down, too?"

Santiago couldn't help but laugh; despite her faded sweatshirt, threadbare flannel pants and messy ponytail, there was a fierce air about Ainsley that only a fool would dismiss.

"We can expose his lies, for sure. And I will personally offer my services to his wife, if she decides to divorce him, after all this is wrapped up. Pro bono, of course."

Ainsley nodded and leaned back, apparently satisfied for now.

"I know you want to help this woman," Santiago said, growing serious. "But please, don't do anything to antagonize Steve. If he sees you as a threat, he might lash out and hurt you."

Ainsley flapped her hand in the air, dismissing his concern. "I'm not afraid of him. I can take care of myself."

"I'm not suggesting otherwise," Santiago replied, digging deep for patience. "I just don't want you to take any unnecessary chances."

Ainsley narrowed her eyes. "I'm not going to turn my back on this woman on the off chance her husband might lose his temper with me. She needs a friend."

"I agree with you." Santiago decided to try a different tack. "But if he's half as bad as we think, he's liable to take his anger out on her."

Ainsley's expression softened. "Yeah, I'm worried about that, too. I told him I wouldn't initiate a conversation with her, but if she talks to me first I'm not going to ignore her."

He could tell her mind was made up. Recognizing the futility of further argument, Santiago nodded. "That seems reasonable." Privately though, he was still worried. It wasn't in Ainsley's nature to walk away from a problem. He could imagine any number of scenarios where she reached out to Jenny, then took the blame if her husband found out they were talking. As far as he knew, Ainsley had never been touched in anger. It seemed as though she simply didn't think it was possible that a man would attack her for speaking to his wife. Unfortunately, thanks to his line of work as a defense attorney, Santiago knew differently.

He watched her now, saw the wheels turning as she tried to figure out a way to help Jenny without tipping off her husband. Admiration filled his chest, but he couldn't shake the twinge of fear for her safety. Ainsley wasn't a rash person—he knew she wouldn't do anything impulsive. But he also understood she wasn't going to stop worrying about Jenny and her situation.

In a way, he was glad she had something to focus on. All the people in his group were unrepentant jerks who lacked the self-awareness of a goldfish. Sitting around listening to these people deny, deflect and blame others for their bad behavior was enough to make him want to tear his hair out. At least Ainsley seemed to have some good people in her group, even though their plights tugged on her heartstrings. At this point, he wasn't sure which scenario was worse: his hating everyone, or her guilt over not being able to save the others.

"What?"

Her question pulled him out of his reverie, and he focused on her again. "I'm sorry?" he asked.

"You have a strange look on your face. What's going on?" she said.

He shook his head to clear his thoughts. "I was just thinking," he said.

She took another sip of coffee. "Penny for your thoughts."

Santiago debated on what to tell her. If he confessed he was worried about her, she'd shrug off his concern and tell him he was overreacting. And perhaps he was. He certainly hoped that was the case. Still, it was probably better he not mention it.

"The baby," he said instead. "I feel bad for their child. I know what it's like to grow up in a home with that kind of tension."

Ainsley's face softened with understanding. "It can't have been easy for you or Gabriela."

He'd told her a little about his family when they'd been dating. It wasn't a topic he liked to discuss, so he tried not to bring it up. But he could tell Ainsley was curious.

"It was tough," he admitted. "I'm lucky, though— I had my sister, so I wasn't totally alone."

"Did you ever learn why your parents hated each other so much?"

Santiago shook his head. "No. And at some point, I stopped caring about the reason. Either figure it out, or split up, you know? Stop torturing the rest of us."

"I bet you couldn't wait to move out."

"As soon as I could," he confirmed. "I tried to take Gabriela with me, but…" he trailed off, remembering the fight. "They told her if she moved in with me, they'd cut us both off financially. At that point, they were paying for my college, and they'd promised to do the same for her. I was willing to go it on my own, but Gabby was afraid. She told me to leave her, that she'd be fine."

Ainsley reached across the table and placed her hand on his own. "How many years did she have until graduation?"

Her touch was soft and warm, and Santiago wanted to flip his hand over and thread his fingers through hers. But that seemed like too intimate a gesture, so he didn't move. Instead, he squinted, searching his memory. "At that point she was a sophomore in high school, so it was two years until she could get out."

"Man." Ainsley shook her head in sympathy. "I can't imagine being so vindictive toward someone I loved."

He laughed, but there was no humor in it. "Oh, that was the tip of the iceberg, believe me."

"Do you think if your parents had done something like this—I mean a real marriage retreat, not this fake garbage—that it would have made a difference in their relationship?"

Santiago considered her question. He'd wondered the same thing from time to time, but had never really come up with an answer. "Probably not," he said. "I think they're determined to hate each other, and nothing is going to change that. I've learned that some people are only happy when they're unhappy, if that makes any sense. I think my parents are like that."

Ainsley nodded. "I think I know what you mean. My father's ex-wife, Selina, is a real piece of work. I'm not sure why they were ever together. Well," she amended quickly, "I'm pretty sure she was only in it for the money, but I don't know what Dad ever saw in her."

Santiago raised one eyebrow, prompting Ainsley to ask, "What?"

"Is she pretty?"

Ainsley scoffed and gently smacked his hand as she pulled away. "Men."

He shrugged. "It's a valid question. I mean, put yourself in his shoes for a minute. His first wife has died, he's got three kids at home and a company to run. A beautiful woman shows up and lavishes him with attention, making him forget the stress of his life for a little while. It's only natural he'd fall for her."

Ainsley crossed her arms. "Is that what happened to you? You fell for a pretty face in New York, someone to distract you from the pressures of the big city?"

Santiago shook his head. "Hardly. I haven't gotten seriously involved with anyone."

"Why's that?"

Because they're not you, his brain supplied helpfully. He shifted in his seat, uncomfortable with the direction of his conversation. Talking to Ainsley was a pleasure, but he didn't want her to know that he still missed her in that way.

"Just haven't found the right person, I guess," he said lamely.

She studied him for a moment, her expression sympathetic. "Are you afraid of turning into your parents?" she asked quietly.

The question hit him like a punch to the gut, an unexpected blow that stunned him for a few seconds. He'd never told her that. Never been able to work up the courage to share the truth with her. Even though it was his greatest fear, he knew how ridiculous it sounded and he hadn't wanted Ainsley to think he was lying to her when he'd left. But perhaps he should have given her more credit.

Santiago struggled to find his voice, knowing she deserved a response. "I haven't exactly had the best role models," he admitted.

"No," she murmured. "You haven't."

Unable to bear her scrutiny any longer, he changed the subject. "What about you?" he asked. "Why is there no ring on your finger?"

Ainsley held out her left hand and looked at it appraisingly. "Actually, there is," she teased.

"You know what I mean."

The smile faded from her face and she shrugged. "Same reason, I suppose. Not the parent thing. The finding the right person thing." She looked down, tracing the rim of her cup with the tip of her forefinger. "Men aren't exactly lining up around the block to date a workaholic who can't have babies."

Santiago's heart cracked at her words. He'd known she couldn't have children—she'd made that clear from the beginning of their relationship. An emergency surgery during Ainsley's childhood had resulted in massive internal scarring, encasing her ovaries and rendering her infertile. She'd always been matter-of-fact about it, and truth be told, he hadn't been bothered by the news. He was attracted to Ainsley for who she was, not for the hypothetical children she could provide. But it seemed that perhaps her outwardly calm acceptance of her condition hid an inner turmoil she'd never shown him before.

"Has anyone ever said that to you?" He tried to keep his voice even, but just the thought of a man making her feel bad because of her inability to have children made Santiago's blood boil. She didn't deserve to be treated like that; she was a vibrant, amazing woman, not someone's broodmare.

Ainsley shrugged one shoulder, not meeting his eyes. "I can read between the lines. I usually wait to tell people until we've gotten to know each other a bit. When they stop returning my calls, I get the message."

He remembered when she'd told him. How she'd seemed nervous and preoccupied. He'd asked her about it, but she'd said everything was fine. Then, in the middle of dinner, she'd set her fork down and announced she couldn't have children.

He could still see the defensive light in her eyes, the way her chin had been turned up, as though daring him to challenge her. He'd asked a few questions and that was that. She'd seemed a little deflated by his underwhelming reaction, but as time had passed, she'd come to accept he'd spoken the truth when he'd told her he didn't need to have biological children.

Was she still at peace with the limitations of her body? Or had something changed?

"How do you feel about it?" he asked softly.

She glanced up, meeting his eyes for a second before looking away again. "I thought I was okay, but as the years have passed, it's gotten a little harder to accept that I can't have kids. When I was younger, I thought I wouldn't care. I'd create this amazing career and fill my life with friends and dogs. But the older I get, the more I feel like I'm missing out." Her hands tightened on the cup, her knuckles going white. "I see my friends having kids and I wonder what it's like."

"You can still be a mom, if that's what you want," he said. "There's always adoption, or perhaps IVF."

"Yeah." She nodded. "I've considered that. I guess part of me is just curious to know what it's like to be pregnant and to give birth. To have this new little person that is a part of me, you know?"

"I do." Santiago had wondered the same, from time to time. But in the end, he always circled back to the same conclusion: fatherhood was great, but it wasn't something he felt compelled to do with his life.

"I think I like the idea of children more than I'd like the reality," she continued. "I know I don't have to be a mother to lead a fulfilling life. But I think a part of me will always be curious as to what things might have been like, if I could have gotten pregnant. Kind of like the way I wonder how things would have ended up if I'd chosen to be a doctor or a writer or a chef instead of a lawyer."

Seeking to lighten the mood, he decided to tease her a bit. "Those are some wildly diverse career choices."

She smiled. "They were all on the list when I was a kid. Along with ballerina and cowgirl."

His brain conjured up an image of her now in a pale pink leotard and tutu, the fabric clinging to her curves. *Idiot*, he told himself. But it was too late. His imagination had taken off, picturing her dancing, her body moving in front of him as she treated him to a private show. Unfortunately, he knew all too well what she would look like, as she'd once worn a ballerina costume for a Halloween party in law school. He'd barely been able to keep his hands off her at the party, and once they'd gotten home, she hadn't worn the outfit long enough to treat him to a dance performance.

He shifted in the chair, trying to find a distraction before his body took the mental image and ran with it, all the way to an embarrassing conclusion. "If it's any consolation, you're an amazing lawyer."

She smiled. "You have to say that because I'm helping you."

Santiago shook his head. "You know that's not why."

Ainsley grew serious. "You're not so bad yourself," she said softly. "Why do you think I called you?"

"Because you knew I'd help?"

She shook her head. "I didn't know that, actually. I hoped you would, but I wasn't taking anything for granted."

It hurt to know she hadn't believed him when he'd told her he'd always be there for her, but could he really blame her? It was the kind of thing people said all the time when they were breaking up with someone. But in his case, he'd truly meant it.

"Well, now you know," he said. "It wasn't an empty promise."

Ainsley nodded, her blue eyes luminous from the glow of the overhead light. "Thank you."

Her gratitude made Santiago uncomfortable. He didn't deserve it, for one thing. They were both helping each other, so there was no need for her to feel like she owed him something for taking her brother's case.

Besides, after the way he'd hurt her five years ago, it was the least he could do.

"Don't mention it," he said. "Please. I don't deserve your thanks. You're helping me too, remember?"

She nodded and looked away, breaking the connection between them. "On that note, I'm going to turn in early. It's been a long day."

"I understand," he said. "I think I'm going to do the same. Maybe we can talk about Ace's case tomorrow, after we've both had some rest? I emailed him yesterday. Hopefully he'll reply soon."

"That sounds good." She pushed away from the table and took her now empty cup to the sink. Santiago got to his feet and followed, intending to set his mug on the counter. But just as he reached out, Ainsley turned and moved forward, pulling up short just before she ran into him.

"Oh!" The small sound of surprise escaped on a breath, and she blinked up at him, her cheeks going pink.

"Sorry," he murmured. "Didn't mean to sneak up on you."

"It's okay," she replied, her voice low.

They stayed like that, close but not touching, staring into each other's eyes. *What are you doing?* his brain demanded. *Move!*

On some level, Santiago knew he was playing with fire. He should step back, give Ainsley some space and let her walk out of the kitchen. But his feet wouldn't obey his brain's commands. Being so close to her stilled the restlessness inside of him, quieting the low-level anxiety that had plagued him ever since they'd started this damn retreat of lies. Logically, he understood this proximity to Ainsley was a bad idea. But emotionally?

He needed her.

Ainsley stared up at him, her eyes large and inviting. He saw no trace of fear, no hint of apprehension in her gaze. She made no move to leave, and it wasn't because he had her pinned—she was free to step back, to put distance between them.

If that's what she wanted.

Santiago waited, giving her time to decide. His mind was made up, but he wasn't going to force himself on her. As he watched her, the tip of her tongue darted out to wet her bottom lip. Any other time, he would have taken that as a clear invitation to kiss her. Now, though? He remained still, giving them both one last chance to walk away.

A smile flitted across her mouth, and she nodded

slightly. She reached out and grasped the fabric of his shirt, then tugged gently.

She didn't have to ask him twice.

Santiago dropped his head and fit his mouth to hers. Her lips were warm and soft, absolutely perfect. As soon as they connected, he felt something click into place inside his chest as every cell in his body seemed to sigh with relief.

Yes. This is right. This is what I need.

It was a sensation more than an actual thought, a sense that this woman was his match in every way. His world shifted, as though things that had once been a little off-kilter were now in perfect alignment. It was a powerful feeling, a rush that left him a little light-headed.

Ainsley pressed herself against him, the added contact sending tendrils of warmth throughout his body. Santiago ran his tongue along her bottom lip, coaxing her mouth open.

He'd barely registered the taste of her coffee when the window behind them shattered.

Chapter 7

Everything seemed to happen in a blur.

One minute, Ainsley was sinking into Santiago's kiss, relishing the feel of her curves pressed against his chest. The next thing she knew, there was a crash from somewhere behind her. Before she could fully register the sound, Santiago's arms came around her in a tight embrace and he pulled her to the floor. The back of her head made contact with the tile floor, and she cried out as pain pierced her skull.

"Are you okay?" Santiago's breath was warm on her cheek; she blinked, slowly registering he was on top of her.

"Uh, yeah, I think so. What happened?" Her head was still spinning from the sudden change in position, and the throbbing of her skull made it difficult to organize her thoughts.

"The window." He shifted, his eyes looking past her as he searched for something. "It shattered behind you."

A jolt of alarm shot down her spine. "Were you hurt?" She hadn't felt anything, but she'd been so caught up in the moment it might not have registered. She took a mental inventory now, trying to determine if she'd been cut or injured by flying glass.

Santiago was quiet for a few seconds, apparently performing his own silent survey. "No, I think I'm fine."

He planted his knees on either side of her thighs, taking some of his weight off her. They waited a few more seconds, but the cabin was silent.

"Do you think we're safe?" She felt a little silly whispering, but windows didn't break themselves. Something had caused the glass to explode.

Or someone.

The image of Steve flashed through her mind as she recalled the dark glare he given her before walking away with Jenny. He hadn't threatened her outright, but he'd made it clear he didn't want her speaking to his wife.

Had he decided to underline his warning with a little vandalism?

"I'll take a look," Santiago said. "Stay down until I know it's okay."

Ainsley opened her mouth to protest, but Santiago

looked down and met her eyes. "Just stay down," he repeated, anticipating her objection.

He waited for her to nod before sliding off her. She registered the loss of his body heat immediately, but pushed the inconvenient observation aside. Now was not the time to think about the implications of that kiss, or the direction they'd been heading before the surprise interruption...

Wanting to keep him in sight, Ainsley rolled onto her stomach and craned her neck. Santiago moved cautiously toward the window at the other end of the room, his head swiveling from side to side as he searched for any signs of an intruder or a threat. She held her breath, willing him to remain safe. The chances that someone was out there waiting to take a shot were slim, but she couldn't get Steve's menacing expression out of her mind. Even though he was upset with her, he might lash out and hurt Santiago by mistake. If Santiago was injured because of her actions...she'd never forgive herself.

After an endless moment, Santiago called out. "I don't see anyone." The glass crunched under his shoes as he walked back to her and reached down to help her up. "I think we're safe."

"What happened?" Ainsley kept her hands on Santiago's arms, unwilling to let go just yet. Her stomach still roiled from adrenaline and she felt a little shaky. He was solid and strong, and his closeness provided a reassurance that transcended words.

Santiago seemed to understand her need for touch,

as he drew her close. "I'm not 100 percent sure," he said, looking at the scene at the other end of the room. "As best I can tell, it seems like a tree branch crashed through the window."

"So it wasn't a person trying to hurt us?" *That* was a relief.

"Doesn't look like it, no," he said.

Together, they walked over to the mess on the floor. Ainsley could see he was right—a large branch was hanging half-out of the room, and both the small table and floor were littered with shards of glass and a few pieces of bark and leaves. From this angle, she could see the jagged end of the branch, which looked like it had been ripped off the tree. She reflexively glanced up, but it was impossible to tell which tree the branch had come from.

"That's quite a mess," she said.

"I'll see if I can find a broom," Santiago replied. She released her hold on him as he stepped away. Rather than watch him walk, she turned back to the scene in the kitchen. Even if Santiago was able to find something they could use to clean up, they would need help blocking the empty space where the window had once been.

With a sigh, she walked over to the phone and pressed 9 to dial the front desk of the main building. *Please, not Brett*, she thought silently as she listened to the phone ring. He was one of the last people she wanted to talk to right now, and with her nerves still on edge, she didn't want him coming over to inspect the damage to the cabin.

"Marriage Institute, this is Carmen speaking," answered a woman's voice.

Ainsley identified herself and explained the situation. Carmen tutted sympathetically, and assured Ainsley that someone would arrive momentarily with plywood to cover the broken window and help clean up.

After thanking the woman, Ainsley hung up. Did nothing faze these people? Carmen's chipper tone hadn't varied throughout the call. Ainsley imagined that no matter the reason for her call, Carmen's response would have been the same.

I'm calling because my arm just fell off.

Oh, that's okay! I'll send someone over to help you clean up!

She shook her head at the thought, and Santiago drew up short as he returned to the kitchen.

"You okay?"

"Yeah," she said. "Just got off the phone with the main cabin. They're sending someone to help us."

"Good, because I couldn't find a broom." He held up his empty hands in illustration and moved to stand next to her.

"I'm sure they'll have everything we need," Ainsley commented. "And I know they'll be cheerful about it."

Santiago chuckled. "I take it you spoke with Brett?"

She shuddered at the mention of the man's name. "No. Thank God. It was someone else. But she sounded just as perfect."

Santiago ran his hand down her arm. "Try not to let them get to you. We'll be out of here soon."

Ainsley nodded, knowing he was right. "Let's get started." She gestured to the mess on the floor. "We can at least pull the branch out of the room."

"Good call." They headed for the front door and stepped out onto the porch. As soon as she walked out of the house, Ainsley froze.

Santiago paused on the steps, glancing back with a worried expression. "Hey. What's wrong?"

She shook her head, searching for the words. The whole thing felt very wrong, but she couldn't quite put her finger on why...

Then it snapped into place. She pointed up with her index finger. "This porch is covered."

Santiago glanced at the roof in question and looked back at her. "Yes." He drew the word out, as though he was waiting for her to realize she was being silly.

"That branch couldn't have fallen through the kitchen window on its own." She gestured to the side, where the branch in question still hung from the frame.

Santiago followed her movement, his eyes tracing the lines of the roof and then the window frame. The porch roof extended to cover half of the width of the window, so it was feasible a branch could have fallen from a tree and busted through the unprotected side.

But that wasn't the case here. The wood had clearly punctured the half of the glass that was shaded by the porch, leaving large shards still attached to the side of the frame that was uncovered.

There was only one way to explain that pattern.

Someone had rammed the branch through the window, wanting it to look like an accident.

Santiago looked back at her, his eyes widening as understanding dawned.

"I think you should go back inside."

Ainsley bristled at his words. "And leave you out here alone? I don't think so."

Santiago shot her an exasperated glare and moved to grab the branch. "How did I know you were going to say that?" he sighed. "Come on then, let's get this done quickly."

Working together, they carefully pulled the branch free and tossed it on the ground in front of the cabin. Then they both walked inside to wait for the cleanup crew to arrive.

"So it wasn't an accident," he said softly.

"Nope," she replied.

He nodded, as though this confirmed a private suspicion. "I thought it was strange. There haven't been any storms, and I didn't hear a gust of wind that might have caused the branch to tear free."

"I have seen some downed branches by the running trail," Ainsley said. "Whoever did this probably picked one up there." Given the forest nearby, pieces of wood weren't hard to find. And it was an ideal tool for vandalism—after all, any reasonable person would assume the branch had fallen from one of the trees close to the house.

It was a mistake they'd made at first, until she'd realized things didn't quite add up.

But...who would do this? And why?

Another thought came swiftly, making her skin crawl with revulsion; how long had someone been standing outside, watching them?

Santiago placed his hand on her arm. "Your face—what is it?"

She shuddered. "I just realized, whoever did this was probably standing outside the window, watching us kiss."

A shadow crossed his face. "Yes," he said shortly.

That safe feeling she'd had after assuming this had all been an accident evaporated, leaving her exposed and vulnerable. What other private moments had this person seen? How long had they been spying?

Santiago drew her close once more, wrapping his arms loosely around her. "It's okay," he said, dropping his mouth to her ear. "Whoever did this, they won't hurt you. I won't let them."

She hadn't started to worry about her personal safety yet, but Santiago's assurance helped soothe her nerves. "Should we say something? When help arrives?"

She felt his head move against her hair. "I don't

think so," he said. "It's not like we can trust them, you know?"

"Yeah." Brett's face flashed through her mind, and she tightened her grip around Santiago's waist. She'd been thinking Steve had done this, or perhaps one of the other spouses trying to intimidate them. But what if it was an employee? Maybe the Woodses had figured out she and Santiago weren't really married at all? Perhaps this was the start of a campaign to get them to leave, or worse still, they'd uncovered Ainsley and Santiago's investigation and wanted to scare them into dropping it.

She said as much to Santiago. He stroked one hand down the valley of her spine; she focused on his touch, drawing comfort from the gesture. "That's possible," he said. He was quiet for a few seconds, then spoke again. "What do you want to do?"

Ainsley pulled back to look up at him. "What do you mean?"

His green eyes were clear. "I'm not going to ask you to risk yourself for this project." He reached up to brush a strand of hair behind her ear. "And I don't want you to spend the remainder of the week living in fear that someone is spying on us or going to hurt us. If you want to leave, we can."

His consideration was like a warm balm on her soul, spreading over her and making her feel cherished. She knew how much this investigation meant to him, how passionate he was about helping his sister and the other people who had been conned.

The fact that he was willing to walk away just so she wouldn't be scared showed how much he cared about her.

Even as she appreciated his concern, a small part of her heart ached. Santiago still thought highly of her, that much was clear. But did it really matter? All the affection in the world hadn't stopped him from leaving five years ago.

Ainsley slowly extracted herself from his embrace, being careful not to make it seem like she was rejecting him. That would only raise questions, and she didn't want to let him know that her heart was still bleeding from his actions.

"I'm fine," she said decisively. "I want to finish this. I'm not going to let some coward with a tree branch scare me away from doing the right thing."

Santiago nodded, a smile tugging the corners of his mouth. "I figured you'd be stubborn. But don't be afraid to change your mind—if you decide you're done, we'll leave. No questions asked."

"I won't. I'm going to see this through to the end." She owed him that much, since he was helping Ace. Besides, if she was to walk away now, part of her would always wonder if these stolen kisses and subtle touches would have led to something more. Her heart was already fluttering with the idea of a second chance for both of them. No, staying here would prove those encounters were nothing but blips, moments of weakness brought on by stress and worry. They weren't the beginning of something new, they were a maladaptive coping strategy she had to shake off.

Her brain understood there was no future for the two of them. Santiago had made that clear five years ago, and nothing had changed.

Ainsley just had to make sure her heart got the message.

Santiago flipped his pillow over with a sigh that night, punching it into the shape he liked before flopping back down on the bed.

He should sleep. He knew this. His body was tired.

But his mind wouldn't shut down.

The events of this evening played on an endless loop, a movie reel he couldn't turn off. Making Ainsley's coffee. Talking with her at the table. Kissing her by the sink...

In some ways, he was grateful the window had broken at that moment. He hadn't meant to kiss Ainsley, but once he'd started, he hadn't wanted to stop. And given his determination to keep his distance, kissing her was the last thing he needed to be doing.

It was strange, though. The more group discussions and couple's therapy sessions they attended together, the more he realized how good their relationship had been. Listening to other people talk about the problems in their marriages made him realize he and Ainsley had been lucky—they hadn't argued all the time, hadn't had big, fundamental disagreements about life, the kind that tore a couple apart. He'd never been tempted to cheat on her, and as far as he could tell, she'd never wanted to cheat on him. Compared to these unhappy couples at the retreat, he and Ainsley had had a charmed relationship.

It was enough to make him wonder if he'd made the right choice five years ago.

He flipped onto his back with a sigh. On the other hand, perhaps the past seemed so good because he was currently surrounded by people contemplating divorce. After all, happy couples didn't consider breaking up. It was easy to think their relationship had been ideal compared to the stories he'd heard over the last several days.

Though he couldn't deny they had worked well together…still did, come to that.

There was no one he'd rather have by his side this week. Ainsley was the best partner he could ask for; not only was she helping him gather evidence against the Woodses and their cronies, but she provided him with the emotional support he'd unexpectedly needed to continue this deception.

Santiago only hoped he was helping her the same way she was helping him.

Which led him to a new set of worries; now that they knew the broken window had been no accident, was he doing the right thing by keeping them here?

He'd never forgive himself if Ainsley was hurt. He knew, too, that she wasn't going to walk away. She was too stubborn to give in to intimidation, especially now that she'd seen firsthand the people who were being hurt by the Woodses. He could tell by the way she'd talked about Jenny that she had a soft spot for the other woman, and he couldn't blame her.

That didn't mean he wanted her risking her own neck to help. It was one thing to provide moral support and to be there as a friend, even if it annoyed Jenny's husband. But now that someone had thrown a tree branch through the cabin window, Santiago feared the stakes were considerably higher.

There was no guarantee the disgruntled husband was responsible for the act of vandalism, though Santiago didn't know who else it could be. It was possible the Woodses had figured out he and Ainsley were not who they seemed—perhaps they were trying to send a message? Though it must be an awfully subtle one, if that was the case. No, if the Woodses suspected their real motives, he doubted they would bother with something as small as a broken window. They'd simply force them out of the retreat and that would be that.

He doubted it was anyone on their staff, either. The employee who had come out to help clean up was perfectly pleasant, apologizing for the accident, saying it happened sometimes. The young woman had definitely stuck to the script, just as all the other staffers had during the week. And while that made them seem a little…creepy, it also made Santiago think they wouldn't do anything unless the Woodses ordered it. So the idea that an employee had broken the window didn't make sense, either.

Which brought him back to Steve, Jenny's husband. He was the only logical suspect so far.

Thanks to the two of them being in the same group, Santiago had seen flashes of the other man's temper. It was easy for him to imagine Steve picking up the branch and thrusting it through the window— it was just the kind of hotheaded, impulsive move men like Steve specialized in. The only question was, now that he'd gotten the anger out of his system for the moment, was he going to leave them alone?

Or would he escalate his behavior?

Santiago wasn't afraid for himself. Steve and his ilk were bullies, only picking on people they viewed as weaker. Even though Ainsley was smarter and stronger than Steve could ever hope to be, she was physically smaller and therefore, in his eyes, vulnerable. That made her an easy target.

And since Santiago couldn't be by her side every minute of the day, it posed a dilemma for him.

Carry on with the operation and risk Ainsley's safety?

Or leave now before someone was seriously hurt?

He knew what he wanted to do. If it was up to him, they'd leave in the morning. As much as he wanted to bring these guys down, to make them pay for their deceptions, the fact was that Ainsley's well-being meant more to him than anything else.

Feeling uncomfortably warm, he flipped the pillow over once more, searching for a cooler spot on the fabric. *It shouldn't be this hard*, he told himself. He didn't want to risk Ainsley, so they should leave. But she'd made it clear she wasn't going anywhere.

And…ultimately, he had to respect her choice.

Even though he hated the risk she was taking, it was hers to assume. He'd do everything in his power to keep her safe, for as long as possible. It wasn't in her nature to rely on someone to take care of her, but hopefully she'd have the sense to accept his help.

Because the only way they were going to get through the rest of this retreat was if they acted as a team.

Chapter 8

At six in the morning, Ainsley decided she'd had enough. Rather than stay in bed, tossing and turning in a vain search for rest, she slipped out from under the covers and began to dress. An early morning run was her usual solution to the problem of an overactive brain. Hopefully, it would work today.

She tiptoed down the hall, careful not to make too much noise. Gentle snoring drifted from behind the closed door of Santiago's room. At least one of them had gotten sleep last night.

The air was refreshingly cool as she stepped onto the porch. She stretched a bit, using the stairs for leverage. Then she set off at a brisk walk under the blue-gray sky.

YOU pick your books –
WE pay for everything.
You get up to FOUR new books and TWO Mystery Gifts,
absolutely FREE!
Total retail value: Over $20!

Dear Reader,

Your opinions are important to us. So if you'll participate in our fast
and free "One Minute" Survey, YOU can pick up to four wonderful
books that WE pay for!

As a leading publisher of women's fiction, we'd love to hear from
you. That's why we promise to reward you for completing our
survey.

IMPORTANT: Please complete the survey and return it. We'll send
your Free Books and Free Mystery Gifts right away. And we pay
for shipping and handling too! ← *We pay for EVERYTHING!*

Try Harlequin® Romantic Suspense books featuring heart-racing
page-turners with unexpected plot twists and irresistible chemistry
that will keep you guessing to the very end.

Try Harlequin Intrigue® Larger-Print books featuring action-packed
stories that will keep you on the edge of your seat. Solve the crime
and deliver justice at all costs.

Or TRY BOTH!

Thank you again for participating in our "One Minute"
Survey. It really takes just a minute (or less) to complete the
survey… and your free books and gifts will be well worth it!

Sincerely,

Pam Powers

Pam Powers
for Reader Service

"One Minute" Survey

GET YOUR FREE BOOKS AND FREE GIFTS!

✓ Complete this Survey ✓ Return this survey

1 Do you try to find time to read every day?
☐ YES ☐ NO

2 Do you prefer stories with suspenseful storylines?
☐ YES ☐ NO

3 Do you enjoy having books delivered to your home?
☐ YES ☐ NO

4 Do you find a Larger Print size easier on your eyes?
☐ YES ☐ NO

YES! I have completed the above "One Minute" Survey. Please send me my Free Books and Free Mystery Gifts (worth over $20 retail). I understand that I am under no obligation to buy anything, as explained on the back of this card.

☐ I prefer Harlequin® Romantic Suspense 240/340 HDL GNUS

☐ I prefer Harlequin Intrigue® Larger Print 199/399 HDL GNUS

☐ I prefer BOTH 240/340 & 199/399 HDL GNWG

FIRST NAME | LAST NAME

ADDRESS

APT.# | CITY

STATE/ PROV. | ZIP/POSTAL CODE

READER SERVICE—Here's how it works:

Accepting your 2 free books and 2 free gifts (gifts valued at approximately $10.00 retail) places you under no obligation to buy anything. You may keep the books and gifts and return the shipping statement marked "cancel." If you do not cancel, approximately one month later we'll send you more books from the series you have chosen, and bill you at our low, subscribers-only discount price. Harlequin® Romantic Suspense books consist of 4 books each month and cost just $4.99 each in the U.S. or $5.74 each in Canada, a savings of at least 13% off the cover price. Harlequin Intrigue® Larger-Print books consist of 6 books each month and cost just $5.99 each for in the U.S. or $6.49 each in Canada, a savings of at least 14% off the cover price. It's quite a bargain! Shipping and handling is just 50¢ per book in the U.S. and $1.25 per book in Canada*. You may return any shipment at our expense and cancel at any time — or you may continue to receive monthly shipments at our low, subscribers-only discount price plus shipping and handling. *Terms and prices subject to change without notice. Prices do not include sales taxes which will be charged (if applicable) based on your state or country of residence. Canadian residents will be charged applicable taxes. Offer not valid in Quebec. Books received may not be as shown. All orders subject to approval. Credit or debit balances in a customer's account(s) may be offset by any other outstanding balance owed by or to the customer. Please allow 3 to 4 weeks for delivery. Offer available while quantities last.

When she reached the trailhead she started to run, taking off down the dirt path that led into the trees. It was darker in the woods, the large branches overhead blocking the tendrils of sunlight that had begun to peer over the eastern horizon. A few enterprising birds were getting an early start to the day, but aside from their tentative songs, it was quiet.

The path was soft underfoot, absorbing the sounds of her steps. She focused on the rhythm of her breathing and let her mind wander.

The kiss last night had been a mistake. Her brain knew it, even as her body denied the truth. This retreat was turning out to be more difficult than she'd expected. Not just because of the Woodses and their con, though she did feel terrible for innocent people like Jenny. No, it was Santiago's presence that she found troubling.

He hadn't done anything objectionable—he was an honorable man, and she trusted him. But being around him every day, sharing the cabin together, the couple's sessions…she was having a hard time resisting the pull of their familiar groove. Without realizing it, she'd fallen into a shared closeness with him, like putting on a favorite pair of jeans. He fit in her life, just as he had before.

And the worst part? Ainsley had thought she'd moved on after their breakup. In many ways, she had. But being around Santiago made it clear there were things still missing from her life. Something as simple as having someone to talk to in the evenings. In a matter of days, Santiago's presence had expanded to fill the cracks in her life, making her aware of the missing pieces for the first time.

She jumped over a fallen tree, the obstacle slowing her down for a few steps. Her heart pounded in her ears as she picked up the pace again, and her thoughts turned back to Santiago.

Why wasn't she angry with him? He'd left her five years ago, using the age-old excuse of "it's not you, it's me." No one would blame her for still being upset—with just a few words, Santiago had crushed her dreams for their future and caused her to question their past. But when Ainsley searched her heart, she found no resentment toward him.

Maybe it was because enough time had passed that the wounds to her heart had healed. Or maybe it was because he hadn't hesitated to help when she'd called.

Or maybe, just maybe, it was because he was still single.

The last possibility was the most dangerous. Why should she care if he was with someone else? She had no claim on him. But the truth of the matter was that she did care.

A lot.

Even though Santiago had assured her he was leaving for the sake of his career, a part of Ainsley had wondered if he was really dumping her because of her infertility. She'd sat with that thought for the past five years, imagining him finding a woman, marrying her and having a houseful of cute babies.

Except, he hadn't done that. And the fact that he was still single and without children forced her to re-evaluate things. It seemed he had told her the truth—it wasn't her after all.

Ainsley made the last turn and slowed to a walk, wanting to cool down a bit before returning to the cabin. The more she thought about the situation, the more she wondered about Santiago's reasons for leaving. He'd built a successful career, yes. But had he really expected her to hold him back? Or was there something more that had caused him to leave?

Leaved crunched under her feet as snippets of last night's conversation floated through her mind…

I haven't exactly had the best role models.

She'd known his childhood had been tumultuous. He'd talked about it in bits and pieces while they'd been dating, but he'd never gone into much detail. Just enough for her to know his parents should never have stayed married.

Was that the problem? Did he think he was doomed to repeat his parents' mistakes?

It made a certain kind of sense. Growing up with miserable parents had to have affected him and shaped his ideas about what a marriage looked like. But she'd foolishly thought that their own relationship had been proof enough that not every couple was doomed to fail.

Now she realized she'd been wrong.

She'd asked him last night if he thought he was worried about turning into his parents. He'd dodged the question, but she could read between the lines. It was clear now that Santiago had left because of his fears, not because of her physical shortcomings.

The realization brought relief, along with a profound sense of peace. She stopped in the middle of the trail and bent at the waist, exhaling heavily as tears sprang to her eyes. For the last five years, she'd doubted the truth of his words, convinced he'd been trying to spare her feelings. Her fears had eaten away at her self-esteem like an acid drip on her soul, triggering a constant, low-level ache that she'd believed was just going to be a part of her life.

But now she saw the truth. And the doubt and heartache brought on by years of second-guessing drained out of her, leaving her feeling both empty and new.

She crouched on her heels and let the tears come, let them wash away the toxic emotions she'd been unknowingly carrying for so long. Ainsley had never been much of a crier, but these tears were cathartic, a fitting end to this chapter of her life.

She wasn't sure how long she stayed there, watching her tears speckle the dirt beneath her feet. Eventually, she stood and wiped her cheeks. Her nose was stuffy and her eyes felt swollen, but it was nothing a hot shower couldn't fix.

Dawn had broken during her run, and from this distance, it was easy to see the plywood covering the broken panes of the kitchen window. Ainsley started walking back to the cabin, hoping Santiago was still asleep. If he saw her face, he'd immediately know she'd been crying. At the moment, her emotions were still close to the surface and she wouldn't be able to deflect his inevitable questions.

She had questions of her own. Like why he'd never told her about his fears before. Why he hadn't trusted her with that information. Maybe they could talk about it now, since they were no longer a couple. It wouldn't change the past, but it would help her understand his actions.

The plywood was a blight on the front of the cabin, its unfinished surface a stark contrast to the polished look of the house. Ainsley eyed it as she got closer, expecting to feel a resurgence of the fear she'd experienced last night when the window had been broken. But the emotions never came.

In the face of her recent self-discoveries, the petty actions of last night's unknown assailant seemed unimportant and insignificant. What did she care if the window was broken? She'd just cast off the subtle despondency that had shaded her life for the past five years. The petty actions of a jealous husband were the farthest thing from her mind.

Pushing thoughts of Jenny's husband aside, she circled back to her own concerns. Now that she recognized the truth behind why Santiago had left, what was she going to do about it? Should she try to get him to see that he wasn't his father, and she wasn't his mother? That he wasn't destined to repeat his parents' sad history? Or should she leave the issue alone? They'd had their chance, after all. Maybe they weren't supposed to get another?

Lost in thought, her steps slowed as she approached the cabin. She stopped on the path, standing just inside the tree line. Perhaps she was being silly, but she was reluctant to go back to this temporary home without some kind of plan in place for how she was going to deal with her emotions. There were three days left in the marriage retreat. Three days of close contact with Santiago. Given the effect he'd already had on her, it might as well be an eternity.

How was she going to protect her heart? Even now, she felt it soften toward him as she considered his own misguided assumptions. She knew what it was like to live with mistaken impressions. Could she help him realize the truth—that he could have a healthy, happy relationship?

More importantly, since he'd left due to his fears did that mean he still loved her? They hadn't split up due to an argument or because of the long, slow death of passion that plagued so many couples. There had been real affection between them, genuine love.

Was it still there? Her heart said yes. Her love for him was dormant, perhaps. But salvageable.

If that's what they both wanted.

She tilted her head to the side, considering her options. But just as she began to organize her thoughts, a noise sounded on the path behind her.

Footsteps.

Ainsley started to turn around, intending to greet the other early morning riser. But before she could complete the rotation, there was a grunt of effort from someone close by and her world exploded in a starburst of pain.

Santiago emerged from his room, the ends of his hair still a little damp from his shower. He walked into the kitchenette and stopped in the doorway, frowning.

Where was Ainsley?

Normally, she was an early riser. She got up at dawn for a run, then returned to the cabin to shower and dress. By the time Santiago was ready to start the day, he usually found her sitting at the small table sipping her coffee.

But today the room was dark and quiet.

He flipped on the lights, started the water for his tea. Maybe she had overslept. It was possible.

But not likely.

Ainsley was a creature of habit. If she wasn't here, then something was wrong.

Hesitating only a second, Santiago walked down the hall and turned right. The door to her bedroom suite was closed, so he rapped loudly on the wood. "Ainsley. Are you okay?"

There was no reply. He knocked a second time, then decided to try the handle.

The door swung open easily and he stepped inside

her room. Morning light streamed in from the window, illuminating the bed with its rumpled covers. He walked through to the bathroom, half-afraid he might find her on the floor. Was she ill?

But the place was empty.

He stood in place for a second, his thoughts churning as a sense of foreboding stole over him. It wasn't like Ainsley to disappear. Even if she'd been upset about something or angry with him, she would have told him if she was going somewhere.

He glanced at the window on the far wall, echoes of last night ringing through his mind. Had someone gained access to her bedroom through the window?

Probably not. It was closed, and the items on the small table that sat underneath the window were still in place.

No, wherever she was, Ainsley had left under her own power.

Was she still running? He glanced at his watch. Normally, she'd returned by now. They usually walked over to breakfast together, and she'd never been late before. But perhaps she'd taken a longer route today? There was an extensive set of trails around and through the woods. Maybe she'd opted for a change of scenery?

That had to be it. Santiago nodded to himself, trying to quash the nerves jangling in his stomach. No sense in imagining the worst when the ordinary was the most likely explanation.

He walked back into the kitchenette and brewed

his tea on autopilot, his mind still focused on Ainsley. Should he go looking for her? What if she'd fallen and injured herself? The trails were uneven, with lots of forest debris like branches and even logs bisecting some of the paths. If she'd tripped or wrenched her ankle or knee, she'd need help getting back.

Abandoning his mug of tea, Santiago set off for the front door. Even though he knew she could have taken any number of routes, he had to at least try to find her. He yanked the front door open and stepped out onto the porch, then drew up short at the sight that greeted him.

Ainsley was stumbling toward the cabin, her hand on her head and her face twisting in pain with every lurching step she took.

"Ainsley!"

Santiago practically jumped off the porch and ran toward her, pulling her into his arms when he reached her. She sucked in a breath at the contact, but didn't pull away.

"What happened? Where are you hurt?" He leaned back and looked at her, noting the dirt on her skin and clothes. He didn't notice any blood, but he hadn't seen all of her yet...

Ainsley winced as she looked up at him. "My head," she said, drawing his attention to her hand, which was still cupped around the back of her skull.

"Did you fall?" It seemed his fears hadn't been unfounded. Moving carefully, he released his hold on her and moved to the side so he could get a better look. She allowed him to remove her hand, but he saw no signs of an injury. With gentle fingers, he brushed past the pieces of dead leaves tangled in her hair and touched her scalp. There was a sizeable lump present, and when he removed his fingers, he saw the tips were pink with a stain of blood.

Ainsley shook her head and winced at the movement. "No, I didn't fall," she said. She met his eyes, her gaze intense. "Someone hit me."

A chill flowed over Santiago, followed swiftly by a rush of heat as anger pumped through his system. "Who?" The word escaped on a snarl, though he already knew the answer.

It must have been Steve, Jenny's husband. Who else could it be?

"I'm not sure," she said. "They hit me from behind so I never saw their face."

Santiago clenched his hands as another wave of anger swept through his body. Not only was Steve a coward who hurt women verbally and emotionally, he evidently attacked them physically—and from behind, as well.

"I see," he said quietly. "Let's get you inside."

Santiago's movements were stiff as he moved to help Ainsley walk the remaining steps to the cabin. His muscles were so tense it felt like they might snap at any moment, but he couldn't lose control. Not now, not while Ainsley still needed him.

She leaned against him as they navigated the stairs. Once inside the cabin, Santiago steered her toward the sofa and she sank down onto the cushion with a sigh.

He knelt in front of her, worry temporarily overcoming his anger. "Are you hurt anywhere else? Do you need a doctor?" There was a disturbing amount of dirt on her clothes, making him wonder if whoever had attacked her had stopped with just a blow to the head. His breath stalled in his chest as he considered additional possibilities, each one worse than the last.

"I think it's just my head." Ainsley gingerly touched the knot on her skull again, wincing as her fingers made contact with the swollen spot. She glanced down and he saw surprise flicker across her face. "Oh man, I'm a mess."

"You must have fallen to the ground."

"I did," she said. "I just didn't realize how dirty I'd gotten."

Convinced she would be all right for at least the next few minutes, Santiago got to his feet. "Stay here," he said unnecessarily. "I'll be right back."

He went to the kitchen and pulled some paper towels free from the roll, then stood at the sink and waited for the water to warm up. He glanced down, surprised to find his hands were shaking.

Santiago dropped his head and focused on his breathing. Deep inhale. Let it out.

Again.

This was getting out of control. The window breaking last night had been bad enough. But now, Ainsley was being physically attacked. It was unacceptable. This had to stop—as much as he loved his sister, Ainsley's safety was worth more than this investigation.

Feeling marginally calmer, he soaked the paper towels in warm water and turned off the tap. Wringing out the excess liquid, he took another deep breath and prepared himself to go back into the other room. He couldn't let his temper get the best of him. The last thing he wanted to do was alarm Ainsley—she didn't need to worry about his emotions while she was hurting.

She glanced up as he approached, a questioning look on her face. He extended the damp towels, and she took them with a small smile. "Thanks."

Santiago sank onto the cushion next to her as she set about wiping the worst of the dirt from her face and the skin of her arms and legs. "We need to call the police."

"What?" Ainsley's head jerked around, making her grimace. "No. We're not doing that."

Santiago felt his jaw drop. "Are you kidding me? You've just been assaulted. Why don't you want to report that?"

"Because." She continued to wipe at the dirt. "If the police show up and start investigating, we'll be exposed. We can't let that happen, not when we're so close to the end of this thing."

He reached out to touch her but stopped before making contact. She was probably bruised from the fall, and he didn't want to add to her pain right now.

But he had to get her attention and make her understand that his personal vendetta no longer mattered. Not when she was at risk like this.

"Ainsley." He waited for her to look at him again. After a moment, she finally met his eyes. "Please, listen to me. I don't care about the Woodses. I don't care about any of this anymore. I just need you to be safe."

"I'm fine."

Her flippant tone made him clench his jaw. "No, you're not. Someone attacked you from behind—I can't ignore that, and you shouldn't either. I want whoever did this to pay." In reality, he wanted to spend a little one-on-one time with whoever had done this so he could work out his frustrations with his fists. His imagination turned up a quick fantasy of beating Steve into submission, an idea that was deeply appealing right now.

"He will." Ainsley's tone was grim. "Look, I know this is bad and getting worse. But it's personal to me now. And I'm not going to give up. I want to take them all down."

Santiago opened his mouth to respond, but she cut him off. "Please." She grabbed his hand and squeezed. "I know you don't like it. I don't, either. But we need to finish this."

His doubts must have shown on his face because Ainsley's expression hardened. "It's my decision," she announced, her tone making it clear she would tolerate no further argument.

Santiago sighed, knowing she was right. He could beg, plead and cajole all he wanted, but in the end, Ainsley was the one who had to press charges. And if she wasn't willing to do so, there was no point in calling the police.

"Will you at least let me take you to a doctor?" That bump on her head felt large, and had to hurt. She could have a concussion, or maybe something worse.

She smiled sweetly. "No." She gave his hand a pat before withdrawing her touch. "I really am fine. Besides, we're going to pretend like nothing happened."

"We are?" This was news to him. What was she planning?

"Yep." Ainsley leaned forward and placed the now-filthy paper towels on the coffee table. "I'm going to take a quick shower, and then we're going to go to breakfast."

"Why—" the word stuck in his throat, so Santiago coughed and tried again. "Why are you doing this?"

Ainsley stood and he noticed a scrape on her knee that he hadn't seen before. "I told you," she said patiently. "I'm going to win this thing. If we act like nothing out of the ordinary has happened, it will drive my attacker crazy. They're bound to slip up and reveal what they've done."

"This isn't a mystery," Santiago protested. "I know it was Steve who hurt you." How could she have any doubts at this point? It's not like there was anyone else it could be...

Ainsley frowned. "Actually, I'm not so sure about that."

"What do you mean?" A chill went down Santiago's spine. Was there something she wasn't telling him? Had someone else threatened her lately?

"I've never seen Steve on those trails," she said. "In fact, Jenny's mentioned in group sessions that he sleeps in all the time rather than helping her with the baby."

"Yeah, but now that they're at this retreat with no baby, his sleeping habits might have changed."

"I don't think so." Ainsley shook her head. "But even if it has, he's not a runner."

"What makes you say that?" Despite his frustration, Santiago was curious to hear her logic. Ainsley's conclusions were generally sound, even though in this case he thought she was mistaken.

"Haven't you noticed his stuffy head and frequent sneezing? Jenny mentioned his allergies are terrible right now. I find it hard to believe he'd choose to spend time outside when he already doesn't feel good."

She did have a point, though it was circumstantial at best. "All right," he said, spreading his hands palms up. "For the sake of argument, let's say you're right. We'll pretend Steve didn't do this. In that case, who did?"

"My money's on Brett," she said promptly. "I think the Woodses use him to intimidate spouses who aren't cooperating with their plans, the ones who resist the gaslighting and manipulation. He makes them feel unsafe and uncertain, making them more susceptible to the Woodses and their suggestions."

"They probably act like nothing is going on," Santiago said slowly, thinking out loud. "Brett terrorizes the spouse, but everyone around them acts like nothing is happening."

Ainsley nodded. "So they think they're going crazy. They can't trust their own perceptions. Maybe they really would be better off alone? And they're getting such a good deal..."

A little shock went through Santiago as he realized she might be right. "I can believe that," he said. "But in your case, you've been attacked. You have injuries that prove you were assaulted. You can't talk a person out of physical signs like that."

"True, but I never saw who hit me," she pointed out. "I imagine if I said something, they'd tell me I'd been hit by a falling branch. And since I didn't actually glimpse anyone behind me, I can't deny it's possible. If I were on my own here, with a husband who was actively trying to get rid of me, isolated from other people... I might question my own reality."

"My God," Santiago whispered. "I think you're on to something."

She smiled wryly. "Don't act so shocked."

He shook his head. "I just can't believe it. Every time I think these people couldn't go any lower, they find another level."

"Now you see why I'm not going to walk away.

We're going to finish this and nail these bastards, once and for all. If we made a stink now, they'd find some way to get out of it and go back to hurting innocent people. We can't let that happen."

Santiago nodded, a renewed sense of determination filling him. "You're right," he said simply. How had he gotten so lucky? How had he picked the one woman in the world who was determined to see this through to the end, despite the personal cost?

More importantly, would he ever be able to repay her?

Ainsley nodded, satisfied with his response. "Just do me a favor," he said as she turned to go.

She glanced back. "What's that?"

He got to his feet, bracing for the battle his request was sure to provoke. "No more early morning runs alone. In fact, no more going anywhere alone."

Her brows drew together and she took a breath. He held up his hand, forestalling her objection. "Ainsley, you got lucky this morning. That bump on your head could have been something much worse. Next time, it will be. Please don't put yourself in danger. I'm begging you."

Her eyes softened and she finally nodded. "All right," she said quietly. "We'll stick together from here on out." She started walking away, then paused at the door. "I guess that means you'll be getting up early, because I'm not about to start skipping my morning run."

Even from this distance, he could see the mischievous glint in her eyes. He let out a dramatic sigh, knowing it was the reaction she was looking for. "Must you torture me, woman?"

She laughed, the sound curling in his chest and warming his heart. "Oh yes. And I'm going to enjoy every minute of it."

Chapter 9

Ainsley let the hot water flow over her hands, enjoying the soothing sensation for a moment. What she wouldn't give for a relaxing soak in the bathtub! It would be the ideal way to ease the aches and pains she'd been dealing with since this morning's attack, but there simply hadn't been enough time. After convincing Santiago to stay the course, she'd had to squeeze in a shower before they'd headed to the main cabin for breakfast and the start of their day of counseling sessions.

The first group session had just concluded, and Ainsley had taken the opportunity for a bathroom break. She'd tried to catch Jenny's eye during the meeting, but the other woman had repeatedly dodged her. Was that because she felt guilty or embarrassed over what her husband had said yesterday, or was she too afraid to cross him by speaking to Ainsley? Either way, it looked like she wasn't going to get another chance to connect with the beleaguered new mother. Perhaps that was for the best, at least right now. If Ainsley drew too much attention to Jenny, it was possible the Woodses would order Brett to terrorize the poor woman, the same way Ainsley suspected she was being targeted.

She glanced in the bathroom mirror, studying her appearance with a critical eye. There were no signs of the attack this morning, at least not on her face. And as long as no one put their hands on the back of her head, they'd never know she had a big lump under her hair. As far as anyone knew, she was fine. It was just another normal day.

A toilet flushed in one of the stalls behind her, and a young lady wearing the uniform of a Marriage Institute employee stepped out and walked to the sink. She smiled pleasantly at Ainsley as she turned on the tap and squirted soap into her hands.

"How are you this morning?"

Ainsley offered her a polite nod. "I'm fine, thank you."

"Are you enjoying the retreat?"

How to answer that? Ainsley had no illusions that anything she said to this person would remain between them. If she indicated she was experiencing any problems, the information would likely be used against her in some way. So she decided to play it cool, in keeping with what she'd asked Santiago to do earlier.

"I'm learning a lot," she said truthfully.

The young woman smiled and turned off the tap. "That's wonderful!" She reached for the paper towels as Ainsley shut off her own water. After a few seconds, the employee tossed her damp towels into the trash and nodded at Ainsley. "Have a good day!"

"You, too," Ainsley said automatically. Then the words sank in and she frowned, staring after her as she walked away.

Have a good day.

The phrase buzzed around in Ainsley's head, stirring a memory. She strained to identify it, but to no avail.

What was it about those words that bothered her? It was a throwaway phrase, the type of empty platitude people spouted all the time. Totally in keeping with the too-polished, too-perfect behavior of the other Institute employees.

And yet for some reason, the phrase struck Ainsley as disturbing.

She shook her head, wondering if the blow she'd taken that morning had knocked something loose inside her brain. It was silly to be so fixated on such a common, innocent sentiment.

But as the day wore on, she couldn't dismiss the feeling that those words revealed a hidden truth.

She sat through the counseling sessions on autopilot, nodding when appropriate, speaking when expected. But though she appeared fine, her brain was busily trying to figure out where that phrase fit into the bigger picture. She felt like she'd been given a piece of a puzzle, but with no idea as to what the final product was supposed to look like, she didn't have the first clue how to start putting it all together.

Santiago noticed her distraction. "What's going on?" he asked at lunch. They sat by themselves, as usual, their table far enough away from the other couples that there was no chance of their conversation being overheard.

"Something happened in the bathroom today."

He tensed, clearly expecting the worst, so she hurried to reassure him. "I'm fine," she said. Some of the tension left his shoulders and she explained her encounter with the Institute employee.

To his credit, he listened closely and didn't immediately laugh in her face. "I know it's probably nothing," she finished. "But something about that phrase hit me. Like a moment of déjà vu or something, you know?"

"It sounds unsettling," Santiago said. "Have you been able to find a connection to anything?"

She shook her head. "Not yet," she admitted. "But I just can't stop thinking about it."

He reached for her hand on the table, but she pulled away before he could touch her. "We're splitting up, remember?"

Annoyance flashed across his face. "Oh. Right."

"I appreciate the gesture." It was sweet of him to try to offer support. Even though he'd never mentioned it, Ainsley was absolutely certain his father had never emotionally supported his mother. The fact that his first instinct was to try to help her was yet one more reason why she knew Santiago was in no danger of turning into either one of his parents. But now was not the time to share her realizations with him.

"I can't help jog your memory, but I can offer some distraction," he said. "I don't know about you, but I need to get some work done tonight. I don't even want to think about how many emails I have now."

"No kidding," she said. Her own in-box was likely bursting at the seams.

Emails... In-box... Good day...

"That's it!" She sat up and gripped the table, excitement thrumming through her.

Santiago glanced to the side, and she realized people were looking at her. Heat washed over her, concentrating in her cheeks. *Way to be subtle*, she thought.

"Uh, I take it you made a connection about something?" he asked quietly.

Ainsley nodded, unwilling to speak until she was certain she was no longer the focus of the dining room. After a few seconds, she leaned forward. "The email that was sent to the board in January—the one that started this whole mess?"

Santiago nodded. "The message that claimed your brother isn't a true Colton."

"Exactly," she replied. "The email sign-off was just two words—*Good day*."

"Okay." Santiago drew the word out, his tone making it clear he didn't put as much stock in this coincidence as she did.

"There's more," she said. "Have you heard of the Affirmation Alliance Group?"

Santiago frowned. "The name is vaguely familiar. Refresh my memory?"

"It's an organization run by a woman named Micheline Anderson. They claim to be a wellness group, focused on self-help and self-awareness, basically any self-thing you can think of that they can monetize."

"I take it you're not a fan?" he asked dryly.

"Not at all," she replied. "The whole group strikes me as being predatory, a way of taking advantage of people's insecurities to sell them something."

"That sounds familiar," Santiago murmured.

"Exactly." Now that she thought about it, Ainsley wondered if the Woodses knew Micheline. Didn't all grifters know each other, if only tangentially?

"Tell me why this group matters." Santiago's question broke into her thoughts, and Ainsley mentally refocused on the issue at hand. Later, when there was time, she'd explore the possibility of a connection between AAG and the Woodses.

"That email was sent by a member of AAG," she

said, filling him in on the convoluted twists and turns in the police investigation. "Micheline's hands appear to be clean, but I just know she's neck-deep in all of this."

"She sounds pretty shifty."

"Oh, most definitely. And the worst thing? I think she might actually be Ace's biological mother." She described what they knew—that a nurse named Luella Smith had given birth right around the time of Ace's birthday; that both she and her baby had disappeared the next day, ostensibly so she could get specialized medical treatment for her ailing son. Then, nothing. The woman and her child, Jake, had apparently vanished.

"So you think this woman, Luella, switched her baby with the real Colton baby? Why would she do that?" Santiago's frown mirrored Ainsley's own internal feelings regarding this mystery.

"I'm not sure," she admitted. "My father said that when Ace was born, he was in pretty rough shape. They actually weren't sure he would make it, but the next morning, they said he was like a new baby." Goose bumps broke out along her arms as she heard Payne's voice in her head, telling the family story. If they'd only known at the time!

"I think Luella switched the babies out because she thought the Colton baby was going to die. I mean, think about it—if you don't want to be a mother, why not swap your perfectly healthy baby for one who looks like he won't live very long?"

"Except he didn't," Santiago pointed out. "If what you're saying is true, her gamble didn't pay off."

"Didn't it, though?" Ainsley asked. "If this theory is correct, then Luella has raised the true Colton son as her own for all these years. Now's her chance to cash in on the deception."

"And you think Luella and Micheline are the same person?"

Ainsley nodded, pleased he was keeping up. "Yeah. Luella's trail went cold forty years ago, shortly after she left the hospital with 'her' baby. And according to Holden and Spencer, Micheline didn't exist until forty years ago." Spencer's Army buddy, FBI Agent Holden St. Clair, had protected Spencer's sister Bella, an undercover reporter, from threats at a recent beauty pageant. The two had caught a serial killer together—and fallen in love.

"That's quite a coincidence."

"It would be, if I believed in coincidences."

Santiago dabbed at his mouth with his napkin. "It's a good story. And I can tell you want it to be true. But I have to say, right now, it's all conjecture."

Ainsley pressed her lips together. "I know," she said, trying to keep the annoyance out of her voice. Santiago was right—she didn't have any real proof, just a gut feeling that this whole complicated situation was Micheline's fault. Still, she didn't like to be reminded of the fact.

He tilted his head to the side, his expression sympathetic. "Sorry," he offered. "I didn't mean to burst your balloon. I just want you to keep an open mind for other possibilities."

It was good advice, and she wasn't too proud to admit it. "You're right," she said. "I can't let my pet theory blind me to other explanations." Still, there had to be a connection between The Marriage Institute and AAG. When she'd seen Spencer recently, he'd told her about a run-in he'd had with Micheline. The woman had denied AAG was a cult, and had left after saying "Good day." It was a little thing, but sometimes the smallest incidents had the biggest impact.

"What are you thinking?" She glanced up to find Santiago watching her. "I can practically see the wheels turning in your mind."

She gave him a half smile. "I'm just wondering if there's a connection between AAG and The Marriage Institute. When we get back to the cabin, I'm going to text Spencer and tell him my suspicions." It was possible he and Holden could answer that question for her—perhaps they had identified the Woodses as known associates of Micheline?

"You think the staff members are members of AAG?"

"It would help explain their demeanor, don't you think?" she asked. "There's something off about these workers, I've felt it from the beginning. Like they were automatons, rather than actual humans. If they've been brainwashed by Micheline and the

Woodses, it makes sense they'll only act according to their programming."

"Let's say you're right," Santiago said. He took a sip of his water and continued. "Do you think the Woodses share the bribes with Micheline, or are they operating on their own?"

"I'm not sure," Ainsley said. "If they're true believers, I think they'd have to share the profits with her."

"Making her an accomplice," Santiago concluded.

Ainsley leaned back in her chair, letting the repercussions sink in. "This might be bigger than we originally thought."

Santiago nodded, his expression grim. "Yeah. We've got to be careful going forward. If what you say is true, Micheline sounds like a real piece of work. If she gets wind of what we're doing here, she'll feel threatened. I don't imagine she's the type to sit back and let the chips fall where they may."

"Probably not," Ainsley said. If Micheline was in on the bribes, she had a vested interest in keeping The Marriage Institute open for business. She wouldn't appreciate Ainsley and Santiago's efforts to turn off the flow of easy money she collected from them after every retreat.

Did she already know? Was that why Ainsley had been attacked this morning? She'd spent the last several hours thinking Alva and Brody were behind the assault, wanting to scare her into accepting Santiago's terms for a divorce. But what if Micheline was driving the bus? What if the Institute employees reported back to her, and took their orders from her? It was enough to make her already aching head start pounding in earnest.

"Hey." Santiago touched her hand, and she opened her eyes to find him watching her. "I know things seem to be getting more complicated, but I'm still here. And I'm not going anywhere."

Ainsley nodded, not trusting herself to speak. She was grateful for Santiago's presence, and she knew he was the only person she could trust right now. But his words set off a dull ache in her chest. She wanted to believe him when he said he wasn't going anywhere. But he'd left her before. And she knew, once this was over, he'd leave her again.

Only this time, she wasn't going to let him walk away with her heart.

Santiago managed to get through the afternoon without incident, though it took all of his self-control not to confront Steve during their group session. Even though Ainsley thought Brett was behind the attacks, he wasn't quite ready to declare Steve innocent. Especially after the man in question shot him a smug look as the session wrapped up.

"Saw your cabin this morning," Steve said, walking alongside Santiago as they made their way to the dining area for dinner. "What happened?"

Santiago clenched his jaw and forced himself to

respond. "We had a tree branch come through the window last night. Glass was everywhere."

"Yikes. Hope no one was hurt."

Santiago studied the man's face, but saw no signs of either deception or amusement. Perhaps he wasn't responsible after all.

"No, my wife and I were both fine." It felt a little strange, saying the word *wife*. But not in a bad way. If things had been different, he and Ainsley probably would have been married for years by now. And happily so—no way would they have needed this retreat, where relationships apparently came to die.

"That's good. I'm glad no one was injured. Bet it was scary, though."

Now *that* was an interesting remark, and consistent with Santiago's theory that the incident had been aimed at intimidating them.

"It was unexpected, that's for sure."

They reached the entrance to the dining hall. Steve stopped, standing in such a way that Santiago was forced to stop as well. "Accidents are the worst." His gaze was level and steady and full of meaning. "If only there was something you could do to prevent them."

Just like that, Santiago went from calm to enraged. For a few seconds, he forgot how to breathe as white-hot anger consumed him. His muscles tensed, ready to fight. His vision tunneled, until the only thing he saw was Steve's eminently punchable face.

He wasn't conscious of moving. Didn't realize

he had, until he registered Steve leaning back, eyes going wide.

"Threaten my wife again, and I will put you into the ground."

Fear flashed in Steve's eyes, quickly replaced by the gleam of bravado. "You're bluffing." He gave Santiago a once-over and scoffed. "You're a desk jockey. Probably never even thrown a punch in your life. You don't have it in you."

Santiago surged forward and grinned as Steve flinched. "Try me," he said darkly. "Please. Give me an excuse."

Steve held his gaze for a second, then looked away. "Whatever," he muttered. "Just keep your wife away from my Jenny."

"My wife does what she wants, when she wants. I don't try to control her. Unlike you, I'm not threatened by a woman who knows her own mind."

Steve glared at him, but didn't respond. He turned and stomped into the dining room, leaving Santiago standing at the entrance, adrenaline still coursing through him.

Had he really just threatened Steve? It wasn't like him to lose control of his temper; it was even more out of character for him to promise physical violence. Normally, he fought his battles with wits and facts, not his fists. But in Steve's case, he was willing to make an exception.

No one threatened Ainsley. Not as long as he was around. Aside from his sister, she was the most important person in his life. He wasn't about to stand by and let some bully take his anger issues out on her.

And if that meant he had to protect her with his body, then that's what he'd do.

He took a deep breath, feeling some of his anger ebb out on the exhale. It was strange, the feeling of anticipation that had come over him, along with the willingness to strike out at another human being. It was a rush like he'd never experienced before. No wonder some men seemed to like fighting—he could see how the endorphin rush might become addicting.

Motion in the dining room caught his eye, and he focused to see Ainsley giving him a wave. A small shock went through him as he realized he was still standing in place, as though rooted to the spot. With a little shake, he cast off the last of this strange mood and walked in to meet her.

Should he tell her about his conversation with Steve? She might want to know their first guess had been correct, at least as far as the window was concerned. Santiago didn't think Steve had attacked her this morning—he wouldn't have been able to keep from bragging about it if he had.

But as he approached the table and saw the fine lines of strain around her eyes, Santiago decided not to share this information. It would only upset her, and if he told her how he'd threatened the other man, she'd worry about his response and fret about the likelihood of his flying off the handle. The last thing he wanted was to add to the stress in her life. He was supposed to protect her, not add to her problems.

"Everything okay?" she asked as he sat across from her.

He smiled. "Yeah. Just lost in thought out there."

"I saw you talking to Steve." She took a sip of water, watching him carefully. "Did he have anything important to say?"

Santiago shook his head. "Not at all. Just bluster. He's not worth your energy."

"That's good." Relief flashed across her face, and he realized he'd made the right decision. "How were your sessions? Learn anything new?"

They fell into an easy conversation, sharing the events of their respective afternoons and moving on to other, more pleasant topics. She was so easy to talk to—she always had been. It was a characteristic he'd taken for granted during their relationship. Fortunately, he was older and wiser now.

He watched her face as she spoke, tracked the play of emotions across her features. Everything about her interested him—her thoughts, her reactions, her emotions. Would he ever grow tired of talking to her? Was that even possible?

She smiled, and he couldn't help but smile in return. Had his parents ever felt this way? Had his father ever sat across from his mother and gotten lost in her smile, felt himself drowning in the depths of her eyes? Had his mother ever looked at his father and felt a warm glow in her chest? Had they ever, in the history of their relationship, loved each other?

He wanted to hope so, for their sakes.

But even if they had started out with affection, somewhere along the way, they'd lost it. The same fate would have awaited him and Ainsley, had they stayed together. And even though he still loved her, he didn't trust the future. No one in his family had ever been lucky in relationships. As much as he wished otherwise, Santiago knew he wasn't special enough to be the exception.

And in the end, wasn't it better to be lonely than to hurt the person you loved?

Chapter 10

Something was going on with Santiago—Ainsley could tell by his demeanor. He smiled and kept up with their conversation, but his body language was a little stiff, and there was a note of reserve in his voice that told her he was worried. Perhaps it had to do with Steve. She'd watched the two of them as they'd stood in the doorway, and she'd seen Santiago's anger rise to the surface. For a few seconds, his normally calm and cool demeanor had disappeared as rage had bubbled up. When he'd suddenly jerked forward, she'd half stood from her seat, convinced he was about to start using his fists. But based on his reaction to Steve's flinch, Santiago had only been trying to intimidate the man.

It wasn't like Santiago to use his height and his body to scare someone. For him to do so now meant Steve had done something to truly anger him.

The window, she thought. *Steve's the one who broke the window.*

No wonder Santiago was upset—either one of them could have been hurt last night, thanks to Steve's temper tantrum. Had he also attacked her this morning?

She studied Santiago's face as they walked back to the cabin together. *No*, she decided. If Steve had hit her with the branch, he would be stupid enough to brag about it. And if Santiago had heard that, he wouldn't have pulled any punches. She would have had to peel him off the other man, and they would be sitting in a police station giving their statements, rather than walking into the cabin.

She waited for Santiago to close and lock the door before sharing her revelation. "It was Steve, wasn't it? He broke the window."

Santiago's body went still, reminding her of a deer caught out in the open. "How did you know?"

"I saw the two of you talking before you came into the dining hall. It's not like you to lose your temper the way you almost did. I figured Steve had said something to set you off, and I figured the window was the reason."

Santiago nodded. "He basically admitted to it, then issued a thinly veiled threat. I don't know what came over me, but in the moment I was angry enough to hit him." He sounded puzzled by his own reaction, an academic trying to apply logic to an emotional situation.

"But you didn't," she pointed out.

"No. I didn't. Probably for the best." He grinned at her. "He's definitely the type to press charges."

"Oh yeah," Ainsley agreed. "Speaking of charges, do you think he's the one who hit me this morning?"

Santiago shook his head. "I wondered that myself, but based on what he said, I don't think so. If I had any doubts, I'd probably be in jail right now for attempted murder."

His words confirmed her earlier thoughts, making her even more convinced Brett was her mystery morning attacker. "I'm glad that's not the case," she said, trying to lighten the mood. "I already have one man in my life in trouble with the legal system. Let's not make it two."

Santiago chuckled. "It would be hard to help your brother from behind bars."

"Do you still want to talk about the case tonight?"

"Absolutely. Are you sure you feel up to it?"

Ainsley nodded. "Yes. But I want to take a bath first. I'm a little achy from this morning, and I think the hot water will help with that."

A dark expression flashed across Santiago's face at the mention of her attack. "Of course," he said. "Take your time. I'll get set up here, and I'll have a cup of decaf coffee waiting for you when you get out."

Ainsley groaned in anticipation. "That sounds wonderful. I shouldn't be long."

She headed for her bedroom, closing the door behind her with a soft snick. Then she walked into the bathroom and turned on the taps.

The water ran as she undressed. She fired off a text to Spencer, asking about a connection between Micheline and the Woodses. Then she ran her hand under the water to check the temperature: it was hot, exactly the way she wanted it. Ainsley sat on the edge of the tub and added a dollop of bath gel, smiling at the resulting explosion of bubbles. Once the tub was full, she switched off the water and slipped inside, leaning back with a sigh of pleasure.

The heat felt amazing on her tired, achy muscles. She closed her eyes and let her mind wander as the bath worked its magic, the warmth of the water radiating down to her bones.

Two days. That's all that was left of the retreat. Forty-eight more hours of putting on a mask and pretending like she and Santiago were a couple in trouble, of acting like she didn't know the Woodses were con artists hurting innocent people.

She wouldn't miss it, that much was certain. It was hard being so passive, seeing a crime happening in real time but doing nothing to stop it. Sure, in the larger scheme of things she and Santiago were doing the right thing. But all the micro-insults, the little digs at people like Jenny, were wearing on her soul. Ainsley had the benefit of knowing she was a target, so it was easy for her to dismiss the suggestions that she was wrong, or that Santiago would be better off without her. But the other people in her group didn't have that advantage. They were internalizing everything the counselors said, blaming themselves for the problems in their marriages, even though their spouses were the ones who had created this particular situation. Only the knowledge that she and Santiago were going to expose the dishonest actions of everyone—the Woodses and the bribing significant others both—kept her going.

But…there were some things she would miss about this week. Spending time with Santiago again had been wonderful, even though the circumstances had been less than ideal. They'd made the best of it, though, falling into a routine of sorts. It wasn't the same rhythm their lives had taken on when they'd been together, but it still felt familiar. She'd grown to enjoy their evening talks, of hearing more about his work and how his career had taken him from New York City back to Phoenix. While she wouldn't trade her work at Colton Oil, it was interesting to learn about the variety of clients Santiago had dealt with over the years.

He still felt like her other half. The time they'd spent apart hadn't changed that. The problem was, she didn't know what to do with this information. Based on things he'd said recently, it seemed his stance on marriage hadn't changed. He truly seemed to believe he was better off alone. While she understood his fears about repeating the mistakes of his parents, she also knew he wasn't the type of man to stay in a bad relationship simply to torture the other person. That took a level of spite that he didn't possess. And while Ainsley wanted so badly for him to understand that, she couldn't make him see the truth.

In the end, it was probably for the best that they were going to go their separate ways after this was over. Being with Santiago again had been a nice reminder of what was possible, with the right person. But as much as it hurt her heart, she had to admit he wasn't for her. Sure, they got along well and were compatible in all the right ways. It just wasn't enough. She wasn't going to beg him to be with her—her pride wouldn't allow it. And since he refused to believe that they wouldn't turn into his parents, well... There was nothing more to be done.

Clearing her mind, Ainsley sank deeper into the water, feeling it brush against the bottom of her chin. Relaxation stole over her as the minutes ticked by. She knew she should finish up and get dressed. After all, she and Santiago didn't have much time left together, and she did want to work on her brother's case tonight while they were still at the retreat and the interruptions of the real world were held at bay.

He was probably still making her coffee, though. She'd get out soon. Just a few more minutes...

He was starting to get worried.

It had been more than an hour since Ainsley had

gone to her suite for a bath. He'd heard the water rushing through the pipes, but that sound had stopped long ago. The cabin was utterly quiet; if he hadn't known better, he would have thought he was the only one here.

Was she okay? He didn't want to disturb her, but his imagination kept creating scenarios that made him worry. Perhaps this morning's blow to the head had left her with a concussion and she'd passed out in the tub? What if she'd slipped getting into or out of the bath and was lying on the floor, out cold?

For the sake of his mental health, Santiago decided to check on her. She might not appreciate the interruption, but he needed to know she was all right.

Giving up all pretense of work—not that he'd been able to focus in the face of his distracting thoughts—he set aside his laptop and got to his feet.

It didn't take long to walk down the hall and arrive at the door to Ainsley's suite. He rapped softly on the wood. "Doing okay in there?"

She didn't respond, so he knocked again, a little louder this time. Still nothing.

Worried now, he tried the handle. It turned easily, and he stepped inside the bedroom.

He paused at the threshold. It seemed wrong to walk in uninvited, like he was crossing some invisible line. But he had to make sure she was okay. As soon as he confirmed Ainsley was fine, he'd leave.

Wanting to respect her privacy, he called out her name before venturing in farther. "Ainsley?"

Still no response. And she should have heard him easily, since the door to the bathroom was open.

Anxiety made Santiago's heart pound. Casting aside all considerations of privacy, he rushed across the room and stepped inside the bathroom, only to draw up short at the sight that greeted him.

Ainsley was reclined in the large tub, the back of her head resting against the wall. Her eyes were closed, her lips slightly parted as she breathed softly. A smattering of bubbles floating on the surface of the water did nothing to hide her curves from his view. Santiago's mouth went dry as he ran his eyes down the length of her body. His hands itched to touch her, to trace her peaks and valleys, to explore her sensitive spots. Would she still feel the same, or would she be a stranger to him now?

He forced his gaze back to her face, guilt flashing through him. She didn't deserve to be ogled, especially when she didn't know it was happening. He felt like the worst kind of voyeur.

Concern warred with shame as he watched her. Was she asleep, or had she passed out due to her head injury? He vaguely remembered watching some medical drama, where the doctor had told a husband not to let his wife fall asleep after a concussion or she might slip into a coma. Oh, was that what Ainsley had done? Had the heat of the water lulled her into a dangerous sleep?

Only one way to know for sure. With his heart pounding against his breastbone, Santiago leaned down and placed his hands on her bare shoulders. He gave her a little shake, hoping she'd forgive this intrusion.

"Ainsley?" he said loudly. "Wake up, please."

He held his breath as he waited for her to respond. When she didn't move right away, he tried again, a sense of despair building in his chest. If something was wrong with her, he'd never forgive himself. He should have forced her to go to the hospital this morning, should have refused to move until she'd agreed to see a doctor...

She stirred in the water, her face scrunching up into a slight frown. Santiago swallowed a yelp of triumph, not wanting to scare her. Her eyelids fluttered open, and she stared up at him.

"Am I late?"

He leaned back and chuckled. "You might say that."

"Oh."

It took a few seconds for her to fully wake up. He could tell she was still groggy as she looked around. "What are we doing in the bathroom?"

"You came in to take a hot bath. It's been over an hour, so I was worried. I came to check on you."

She looked down, seeming to register the water for the first time. "I'm naked."

Santiago's cheeks heated. "Ah, yes. You are."

He expected her to cover herself, but she didn't. Instead, she turned her head and looked him up and down. "Why aren't you?"

Her question was so unexpected it knocked the thoughts right out of his head. "Um...what?"

"You heard me." Her eyes were clear, all traces of sleep gone.

"I... I..." He was reduced to sputtering, his mind frantically trying to keep up with current events. Was he dreaming? Was he imagining things? Or had the blow to her head been so severe it had caused brain damage that was now manifesting in this unusual way?

Ainsley got to her feet and stepped out of the tub, totally unselfconscious about her nudity. She bent to pull the stopper, presenting Santiago with a view that nearly stopped his heart. His blood raced south, making it even harder to think.

She wrapped a towel around her body and took his hand. "Come on." With a gentle tug, she pulled him into the bedroom.

"What is happening here?" he whispered as she pushed him down on the mattress.

She straddled his lap, pressing the heat of her core against the fly of his pants. "I'm tired," she said, rubbing against him. The friction made his eyes roll back in his head, and he gasped for breath.

"The last few days have been so hard," she continued. She licked the side of his neck, her tongue leaving a hot trail that immediately cooled in the air of the room. Goose bumps broke out across his skin and the hair on the back of his neck stood on end.

"I'm tired of hearing about pain. I'm tired of seeing people hurt each other. You're a good man, Santiago. I know you don't see it, but I do. I know we don't have a future, but please, just give me tonight. Help me forget all of this, if only for a few hours."

She cast off the towel, sending it to the floor. Then she took his hands and placed them on her breasts. Her nipples hardened against his palms, and his fingers curled reflexively to cup her.

Everything she said made sense, and echoed his own internal feelings about the retreat. He'd drawn comfort from her presence this week, but perhaps they could give each other more. Maybe she was right—maybe they could lose themselves in pleasure and forget about the world for a little while.

It wasn't the smartest idea, at least where his heart was concerned. Santiago knew that if they slept together, he'd fall back in love with her again. Still, it was a price worth paying. And in a way, he owed her. He would have helped with her brother's case even if she'd refused to attend the retreat. But she was here, and she'd suffered for her efforts. If he could help her he would, even though he knew it was going to cost him.

Still, he had to make sure they were on the same page. He wasn't prepared to offer her something long-term. All he could do was give her tonight. She'd said she understood, but was that just her arousal talking? Or did she truly know he wasn't good for anything but this impulsive encounter?

"Ainsley." Thanks to the roar of blood in his ears, his voice sounded like it was coming from far away.

She leaned back, biting her bottom lip. "Mmm?"

God, she was beautiful! What was he going to ask again...?

She rocked against him and he couldn't contain a moan of need. His thoughts were circling the drain, his brain on the verge of ceding control to his body. Think, he had to think while he still could!

Ainsley placed her hands over his, causing him to tighten his hold on her breasts. "What do you need?" she whispered, her breath hot against his ear.

With the last of his willpower, Santiago slipped his hands free and placed them on her hips, halting her movement. "Are you sure?"

She paused, and he took the opportunity to breathe. She'd asked what he needed from her, and the truth was, he had to know she was certain about this. The last thing he wanted was to hurt her, even inadvertently.

Seconds ticked by, feeling like an eternity. Then she shifted, wriggling back. "I'm sorry. I shouldn't have...you don't want me."

Santiago kept his hands where they were, knowing if he let her go he'd never get her back, not even as a friend. "That's not it," he said, hating the note of hurt he'd put in her voice. "That's not it at all. I just want to make sure you're going into this with a clear head."

She looked at him, her blue gaze steady. "I know what I want. Do you?"

He couldn't help but smile at the subtle challenge in her tone. "I've always known," he said softly. Surprise flashed in her eyes—didn't she know how much he still cared for her? He wanted nothing more than to surrender to the need arcing between them, but he had to make sure they both understood the rules first.

"But you have to know that I can't give you what you want."

A shadow crossed her face. *This is it*, he thought. *She's done.* Disappointment flared in his chest, but he knew he'd done the right thing. Sex with Ainsley had always been mind-blowing, but at least this way he'd still be able to live with himself tomorrow.

To his surprise, she didn't move. She offered him a sad smile, then reached for his hands and put them back onto her breasts. Her skin was chilly against his palms, her nipples hard points he couldn't ignore. "This is what I want. Just you. One night only."

Santiago exhaled hard, the breath gusting out of him along with the rest of his reservations. Truth be told, this was still probably a bad idea. But he'd had worse.

Letting go of his doubts, Santiago dropped his head and took what she was offering.

Chapter 11

Ainsley let her head fall back and surrendered to the feel of Santiago's hands on her breasts and his mouth on her neck. This impulsivity was out of character for her, and it felt equal parts scary and thrilling to ignore the little voice in her head that always preached reserve and self-control. Even now, that little voice squawked in alarm, frantically insisting this was a mistake. And it probably was. But Ainsley was so desperate for Santiago's familiar comfort that she couldn't bring herself to care.

When she'd opened her eyes and seen his face above her, something had clicked deep inside her chest. She couldn't find the right words to describe how he made her feel, but she recognized the sensation: it was like coming home after the end of a long day. It wasn't fair that five years after he'd walked out of her life she still associated him with solace and security, but perhaps that was one of life's jokes.

Despite their years apart, Santiago still knew just how to touch her to drive her wild. His hands moved over her now, squeezing here, caressing there, his fingers skillfully building her arousal with a few well-placed strokes. And his mouth! The heat of it left a blazing trail of sensation across her skin that soon had her writhing in an unconscious expression of need and desire.

Needing to touch him, wanting to know if he still felt the same under her hands, Ainsley fumbled at the buttons of his shirt. Santiago captured her mouth with his own and tried to help her. Their fingers and tongues tangled together as they worked, and eventually, the two halves of his shirt opened to reveal the skin of his chest. Ainsley sighed as her fingertips made contact with the soft hair that dusted his pecs, and her thumbs brushed over his nipples. They hardened beneath her touch and she smiled against his mouth.

Santiago shifted, shrugging off his shirt before touching her again. He slid his hands from her hips to her bottom, cupping her curves with an air of possession that thrilled her. Without warning, he tightened his grip and pulled her up and forward, pressing her against his chest and settling her bare core on top of the bulge in his pants.

Heat suffused her body, the skin-on-skin contact nearly overwhelming her system. Ainsley threaded her fingers through Santiago's hair, loving the feel of it but also needing an anchor to keep her upright. His erection throbbed under her, her sensitive tissues feeling every one of his heartbeats.

Ainsley's need built, the pressure inside her searching for an outlet. Unable to keep still any longer, she rocked her hips, dragging her core along the hard ridge tucked behind the fly of his pants. More, she needed more.

A small whimper sounded from somewhere in the room. With a shock, Ainsley realized the sound had come from her. "Please," she whispered, the word ragged even to her own ears.

"You don't have to beg." Santiago's voice was gravelly, his breath hitched. "You never have to beg me."

He slid his hand between them, working the button of his pants. With every movement, his fingers brushed against her sensitive nub. Ainsley bit her lip and clenched his shoulders, trying to stave off her orgasm. She didn't want to find release until they were joined together, their bodies moving as one.

Santiago's movements were jerky and uncoordinated, his usual dexterity impaired by arousal. Finally, she heard the rasp of his zipper and then she felt his flesh against hers, smooth and hot and hard.

She reached down to position him, but he put his

hand over hers, stalling her movements. Ainsley looked up and found worry in his green gaze.

"I don't have a condom," he said. "I should have thought of it before, but well… I got distracted."

Ainsley shook her head. "I don't care." Pregnancy wasn't a concern for her—doctors had made it clear she could never have a baby, and after the beginning stages of their relationship, they hadn't used protection. She hadn't gotten pregnant then, had never even experienced a scare. It simply wasn't going to happen.

"I know we never used condoms before. I just didn't want you to think I assumed… I mean, it's been a while, and…" he trailed off, clearly at a loss.

"My last round of tests came back normal," she said. "But if you'd feel better—"

"No, it's okay," he said quickly. "My last screen was normal, too."

She smiled at him, touched by his consideration. Under any other circumstances, she would have initiated the protection discussion long before things had escalated to this point. But given their history and what she knew of his character, she trusted Santiago. His display of concern at this charged moment was yet more proof that her trust in him wasn't misplaced.

"That's good to know," she said. She leaned forward and ran the tip of her tongue up the side of his neck, pressing a kiss at the corner of his jaw.

Then she moved to nibble on his ear lobe and was rewarded by his sharp inhale.

Ainsley lightly raked her nails down his chest to his stomach, then wrapped her hand around his erection once more. She rose up onto her knees, but just as she was about to sink down, Santiago gripped her hips.

Before she could ask what was wrong, the world spun and she found herself flat on her back, staring up at the ceiling. "Santia—" His name died in her throat as he moved down her body. She felt his large hands on the inside of her thighs, pushing her legs apart. Then his mouth was on her, his tongue exploring her most sensitive parts with a skill that sent her eyes rolling back in her head.

The tension built in her body with every stroke, a spring coiling tighter and tighter inside her. Ainsley moaned, thrashing about as the sensations buffeted her from all sides. But Santiago never wavered in his attentions. His hands held her in place as he ravished her with single-minded focus.

Unable to hold back any longer, Ainsley stopped trying to control her body and let the waves of pleasure wash over her. The orgasm rolled through her, her muscles contracting and relaxing in a timeless rhythm that seemed to consume her.

She wasn't sure how long it lasted. The satisfaction of completion erased all sense of time and place, leaving her unmoored in an abyss of sensation. Gradually though, she became aware of Santiago's presence.

He kissed his way up her body, his hair tickling her skin as it brushed over her. "I've been wanting to do that since I walked into your office and saw you standing behind your desk." His voice was low in her ear, his tone smugly satisfied.

"What took you so long?" she croaked.

He laughed, the sound sending residual shocks through her core. "My perfect Ainsley, always so prim and proper. Do you know how much I love mussing you up?"

She couldn't find the words to reply. His eyes bored into hers, his arousal making them glow like green fire.

"Do you like it when I make you lose control?"

She opened her mouth to respond, but before she could speak, he slid inside her. She moaned as her sensitive tissues parted to allow his entry, his erection filling and stretching her in all the right ways.

"That's what I thought." He paused, buried deep inside her. His eyes searched her face, his expression one of intense focus. "Did you miss me?" he whispered. "Did you miss this?" He punctuated the question with a little thrust of his hips, touching a spot inside of her that only he had ever been able to find.

"Yes," she gasped, urging him to move with her hands and her hips. But he settled his weight onto her, holding her in place. It was clear Santiago wanted to be in charge, and for the moment, she was happy to let him.

"Good." The satisfaction in his voice was unmistakable. "Because I missed you, too."

Before he'd finished speaking the words, he started to move, his hips settling into a rhythm that was at once familiar and new. Ainsley wrapped her legs around his waist and gripped his shoulders, relishing the feel of his big body over hers. Yes, she'd missed this. He'd always felt like her other half, and now that they were joined together again, her heart was full for the first time in five years. Sex with Santiago had always been more than just a physical experience for her. Their bodies, their breath, even their souls entwined, linking them in a way that transcended time and space. Ainsley had never found this connection with anyone else. For a while, after Santiago had left, she'd wondered if she'd simply imagined it. Maybe her broken heart had conjured it in a fit of desperate loneliness. But now that they were together again, she knew she hadn't been wrong. This man truly was her equal and other half.

She felt him tense above her, knew he was close to his own release. Acting on a combination of instinct and habit, she lifted her head and gently bit his shoulder, pressing just hard enough to leave marks in his skin. He cried out, then shuddered as he found his completion. She held him as his body kicked inside hers, her own core squeezing as she climaxed in response to his passion.

Breathing hard, Santiago lowered himself until he was flush against her. Ainsley welcomed his weight, loving the way he made her feel surrounded and safe and small in comparison. She stroked her hand up and down his back as they returned to earth together.

Eventually, he stirred and lifted his head. "That was…"

She smiled at his shell-shocked expression. "I know."

"You always know just what to do."

"I could say the same for you," she replied, enjoying the compliment.

A look that could only be described as pure masculine satisfaction crossed his face, and she laughed. "Hey, now. This cabin isn't big enough for the two of us and your ego."

He waggled his eyebrows. "Are you sure?"

Ainsley nodded, pleased to see him so happy. The events of this week had put lines of stress around his eyes and mouth, but at the moment, they were gone.

Santiago rolled onto his back and reached for her, pulling her against his side. "That's too bad," he remarked, his hand drifting lazily down her arm. "I always love it when you stroke my…ego."

She groaned at the bad joke, making him laugh. "Oh, come on. It was a little funny."

"Nope," she said, resting her head on his shoulder. "I'm not going to encourage you."

They lay in silence for a time, their bodies growing cool in the air of the room. Ainsley wondered if Santiago was going to leave, but she didn't want to ask the question. She was happy for him to stay, happy to spend the night in his arms, the way they used to sleep together. They'd already broken so many rules tonight; what was one more?

She felt him relax against her, heard his breathing deepen as he slipped into his dreams. A sense of peace stole over her as the seconds ticked by. She reached down and pulled the covers over them, the way she'd done a million times before.

The regrets would come; she knew that. Maybe not tomorrow, maybe not even the day after, but some day she knew she would wish that she'd had the strength to resist falling back into bed with Santiago. Now that she'd slept with him again, reaffirming their connection in every way that mattered, it was going to be that much harder to walk away when this was over.

But she'd worry about that later. Right now, with the man she still loved beside her, Ainsley closed her eyes and drifted off to sleep, warm and safe in Santiago's arms.

It was dawn when she woke, the room growing lighter by degrees as the sun began to peek over the horizon. Ainsley stretched, then froze as she remembered she wasn't alone.

She turned her head, expecting to see Santiago sleeping next to her. But the bed was empty, the rumpled sheets the only evidence of his presence.

Ignoring the ache in her heart, Ainsley slipped out of bed and walked to the bathroom. She turned on the shower and brushed her teeth, pushing down her disappointment. What did she expect? They'd made no promises to each other last night. Both of them had known the score—the sex was a one-off, not the start of something new. Of course Santiago had returned to his own bed to sleep last night.

Still, she couldn't ignore the slight pang in her chest as she washed the last of his scent from her skin. Logically, she understood their encounter had been a moment out of time, a temporary respite they'd created for themselves. But her emotional side wished it could have lasted a little longer. Was a few more hours away from the real world too much to ask? Apparently so.

She toweled off and pulled her still-wet hair back into a ponytail. Then she dressed in running clothes and stepped out of her bedroom suite.

The light in the kitchenette was on. She frowned; Santiago must have left it on last night before he'd come to check on her in the bath. But as she walked down the hall, she smelled coffee…

She stepped into the kitchenette, surprised to find Santiago standing at the counter, his back to her. He was dressed in a T-shirt and sweatpants, and he was wearing an old pair of sneakers. Ainsley drew up short, frowning. Santiago was not a morning person. What was he doing here, and wearing something other than a bathrobe?

He must have heard her, because he turned around and handed her a cup of coffee. "Good morning." His tone made it sound like he met her all the time at dawn with coffee in hand.

"Morning," Ainsley replied, taking a sip from the mug. "I'm surprised you're up so early."

He shrugged. "I told you, we're sticking together from here on out. That means if you go for a run, so do I."

A smile tugged at the corners of her mouth. Truth be told, she'd forgotten about his promise to accompany her. "I didn't think you were serious about that."

"Oh yes. I'm not about to risk you getting attacked again."

The mention of yesterday's events made the back of her head ache, and she reached up to touch the still-tender spot. The swelling was almost completely gone, but she was certain the bruise would linger for a while. "I appreciate it."

He nodded. "I wasn't sure you were going to get up this morning, after…" he trailed off, his cheeks going pink. He cleared his throat and continued. "Anyway, I got up early and took a shower in my bathroom so as not to disturb you. Then I went to the car and dug out an old gym bag I had in the trunk." He gestured to his clothes. "Now I'm dressed for the occasion."

The hurt and disappointment she'd felt at waking to find him gone melted away. He hadn't left because the sex was over and he'd wanted to sleep alone. No, he'd left to get ready to go running with her, if that's what she wanted to do. Santiago might not realize it, but given his dislike of both mornings and running, Ainsley recognized his efforts as a gesture of love.

Warmth filled her chest, suffusing through her body until she thought she might actually be glowing. "We don't have to go." The offer was enough—she didn't want to torture him.

"No, no, I want to," he assured her. "Though we might need to do more walking than running. I don't know if I can match your pace."

"That's okay," she told him. "It'll be nice to just be outdoors."

"I agree." He reached for her cup and put it on the counter. "I usually stick to the rowing machine at the gym, and since there's a shortage of rivers in Phoenix, I never get to row outside. This will be a nice change of scenery for me."

They walked out of the cabin together, and she led him through her usual stretching routine. "Did you row in New York?" He'd enjoyed racquetball when they'd been together, but it sounded like he'd found a new exercise in the time they'd been apart.

"Yes," he said. "There was a club at my firm that I joined shortly after moving there. Seemed like a good way to make new friends, and I actually enjoyed it."

He told her about it as they set off. Ainsley deliberately slowed her pace, prioritizing conversation over aerobic achievements. They fell into an easy flow, the time passing quickly as they ran in unison.

After what seemed like only a few minutes, they were back at the cabin, having finished the main trail loop. In silent agreement, they slowed to a walk as soon as they came out of the woods.

"How'd you like it?" Ainsley asked. Santiago hadn't had any trouble keeping up, thanks to his long legs and his rowing habit. If he wanted to join her again in the morning, she'd push him to go a little faster.

He grinned, sweat gleaming on his forehead. "It was good," he said. "But I think I need different shoes if this is going to be a regular thing."

Ainsley smiled, but inside, she felt a pang at his mention of the future. It was nice to think they could remain like this, lovers who went running together every morning. But that wasn't going to happen. As soon as this retreat was over, she'd go back to her offices in Mustang Valley and he'd go back to Phoenix. Even though the two cities weren't that far apart, they might as well be in different galaxies.

Still, she wasn't going to let future pain rob her of her current joy. So she pasted on a smile and patted his shoulder. "Don't worry," she said. "I packed a few bandages. With a little TLC, your blisters won't last more than a few days."

"Does this mean we can take the morning off tomorrow?" He sounded so hopeful Ainsley couldn't help but laugh.

"Not a chance," she told him.

Santiago shook his head, but she saw the glimmer of amusement in his eyes. "I'll get you back for this, just you wait."

Heat flared to life in her belly as she heard the unspoken promise in his voice. "Is that right?"

"Oh, yes," he said, his voice warm and low. "I have all kinds of ideas."

"Is that right?" She leaned against his side as they walked, needing to touch him. "What'd you have in mind?"

"It would take too long to explain." Santiago dropped his head, his breath warm across her ear. "I'll just have to show you."

Goose bumps broke out along her arms and legs, and Ainsley shivered in anticipation. Santiago must have felt the movement, because he chuckled with satisfaction.

"You tease," she said.

He put his arm around her shoulders and pulled her in closer. "It's only a tease if I don't follow through. But I have every intention of keeping my word."

A growing sense of arousal sent tingles through her breasts and core. She knew from experience, both historical and recent, that Santiago was an inventive lover. She hadn't expected their reunion would last longer than one night, but she wasn't opposed to the idea, either. It sounded like Santiago felt the same way.

"Morning, folks."

The new voice broke into their private moment, and the pair of them drew up short. Ainsley turned to find Brody Woods standing on the porch of their cabin, eyeing them speculatively.

"Brody, what a surprise." Santiago dropped his arm from her shoulders and stepped forward to shake the man's hand. "What brings you to our cabin this morning?"

"I wanted to check out the damage from the broken window and make sure the temporary repair was taking care of things for you," he said. "I would have come out sooner, but we've been so busy I haven't had a chance."

"I understand," Santiago said smoothly. "As you can see, the plywood is keeping out the raccoons."

Brody laughed, though it sounded a little forced. "Good, good. Seems the window people won't be able to come out and replace it until Monday, which means you folks are going to have to deal with this eyesore for the rest of the retreat."

"That's okay," Ainsley said. "We can live with it for the next forty-eight hours."

Brody looked her up and down, his eyes lingering a little too long on her bare legs. "That's good," he said, sounding somewhat absent. "I was sorry to hear about the accident. Bet it was scary for you."

"It was unexpected," Santiago said, stepping to

the side as if to partially block her from Brody's view. "But your employee was most helpful with the cleanup."

Brody shook his head slightly, as though to clear his mind. "Glad to hear it," he said. "I'll leave you two now. Got to get back to the big house. We've got a special speaker today at lunch, and Alva needs my help to make sure everything's ready."

"Oh?" Ainsley said. "What's the topic?"

"Being Your Best You," Brody said.

A chill shot down Ainsley's spine at his reply. "That sounds interesting," she said, hoping she didn't sound as wooden as she suddenly felt.

Brody nodded. "It is. Micheline is a fantastic speaker. You guys are going to love her."

"Can't wait," Santiago said.

Brody stepped off the porch and walked past them. Santiago offered Ainsley his hand and led her up the steps. "Breathe," he instructed quietly.

She waited until he'd shut the door behind them. "I knew it!" she exclaimed, spinning around to face him. "I told you they're connected."

"Probably," Santiago agreed. "But we have a more immediate problem—does Micheline know who you are?"

"You mean, will she recognize me if she sees me?" Ainsley asked. Santiago nodded.

"I'm not sure," Ainsley said. "I've seen her a few times around town, but we've never been officially introduced. Still, she probably knows I'm Ace's sister, and she definitely knows some of my other family members."

Santiago's expression was serious. "What do you want to do?"

Ainsley considered the question, mentally reviewing her options. They could both leave, today, before Micheline saw her and blew their cover with the Woodses. But they were so close to the end of the retreat, and with the couples all slated to share their decision to stay together or split up tomorrow during the closing session, they needed to stick this out. It was the final piece of evidence they wanted to connect the bribes and the retreat outcomes, and Ainsley didn't want to walk away without getting it.

"Why don't you go to the seminar?" she suggested. "I'll pretend to have food poisoning, so they won't suspect anything. That way, we'll still be able to finish the retreat."

"Are you sure? I don't like the thought of leaving you alone."

"I'll be fine," she assured him. "I'll hang out here and lock the door. Nothing to worry about."

She could tell by the set of Santiago's mouth that he didn't agree with her, but he didn't argue. "All right," he said. "What about this morning? Are you going to attend the morning sessions, or would you rather stay here?"

"No, I'll go," she said. "The counselors are really

putting on the pressure now that we're so close to the end. I need to record all the evidence I can get."

"Okay." Santiago nodded in agreement. "Let's get cleaned up, then. We've got work to do."

Chapter 12

The news that Micheline was making an appearance at the retreat had put a damper on the morning. But despite this unforeseen complication, Santiago still walked into his first group counseling session with a spring in his step. It wasn't just last night's sex or this morning's run that had put him in a good mood, though he couldn't deny that both activities had been thoroughly enjoyable. No, he was riding the residual high of having fully reconnected, physically and emotionally, with Ainsley.

Santiago was happy to be with her now. In some ways, the knowledge that this liaison was temporary felt freeing, and allowed him to fully enjoy their chemistry. He'd be sad when the retreat ended and they went their separate ways, but that didn't mean they couldn't appreciate each other's company now. If only they'd surrendered to the attraction earlier in the week! They could have had more time together, rather than the scant hours they had left. But it was probably better this way, he told himself. Walking away from Ainsley was going to hurt, he knew that. If they'd started sleeping together on day one of the retreat, he probably wouldn't have been able to let her go again when this was all over.

Brody sidled up to him as the first session ended. "You and the missus looked awfully cozy this morning," he remarked.

Warning bells started clanging in Santiago's head. Brody sounded nonchalant, but Santiago recognized his comment was more than just a casual observation.

"Did we?" Santiago replied. He shrugged, as if he didn't care one way or another.

"Mmm-hmm." Brody waited until the rest of the group had cleared the room. Then he fixed Santiago with a dark stare. "Have you had a change of heart since we last spoke? Because I can tell you, if you have, you're not getting your money back."

Santiago's heart kicked into a higher gear and he sent up a silent prayer of thanks to the universe that he hadn't yet shut off his hidden camera. The spy cam around his neck was picking up everything, and at this point, Brody was only deepening his own grave. This evidence, combined with the research one of his paralegals was doing into the financial records of the Woods and The Marriage Institute, would make the case against the Woods air-tight. As soon as he heard from his paralegal, he was going to contact the police and give them all the evidence.

"I haven't changed my mind," Santiago replied. "But from what I've seen this week, it'll be easier to get her to initiate the divorce if she thinks we're going to part as friends. Isn't that what you've taught us? To play nice until we get what we want?"

Brody nodded. "That's true. But most people aren't that good at acting the part. You need to be careful. I could tell by the way she was looking at you that your wife still loves you."

The observation landed like a blow, and for a second, Santiago couldn't breathe. Ainsley had told him last night that she knew this wasn't going to turn into anything. He'd believed she was telling the truth, had convinced himself it was okay to sleep with her because she wasn't going to let herself get hurt.

But had she been lying? Not to him, but to herself?

Was he going to break her heart all over again?

He forced himself to smile, hoping he didn't look as pained as he felt. "Trust me, Grace knows the score." It felt strange to use Ainsley's middle name, but he had to keep their cover intact for a little while longer. "My wife is aware that we don't have a future together." He hated saying the words aloud, and especially to this man, a relative stranger who had no business hearing about their relationship, fake or not.

Brody looked skeptical. "If you say so. Just remember, we told you there are no guarantees. If she doesn't sign the papers, it's not our fault."

"I understand," Santiago said, trying to hide his disgust. Brody and Alva were even worse than he thought! If they truly cared about people, they'd be happy to see one of the couples at the retreat looking stronger and more connected. Instead, they were only worried about their bottom line and the possibility he might demand his bribe money back. Taking them down was going to be one of the most satisfying moments of his career, possibly even his life.

Brody nodded. "I'll check in with Alva, see what she's been saying in her group sessions. Hopefully you're right, and she really is getting ready to let go of your marriage."

Santiago wanted to protest the invasion of Ainsley's privacy, but he stopped himself just in time. For one thing, it didn't really matter since they weren't married and she was playing a part to help him. She hadn't been baring her soul in the group sessions, so he didn't have to worry about learning any secrets. Also, he had to keep his own role in mind: a husband who bribed the coordinators of a marriage retreat and asked for their help to convince his wife to get a divorce was not the kind of man who would worry about his spouse's privacy in the first place.

"That'd be great," he said instead. "I definitely

don't want any surprises, especially so late in the game."

Brody clapped him on the back with a friendly smile. "We don't either, son. Now, get on to your couple's session. I'm sure she's waiting for you."

Ainsley left the room where the group session had just been held and stepped into the hall. She was due for a couple's session with Santiago in a few minutes, but after one too many cups of coffee this morning, she needed a bathroom break first.

She stepped into the restroom and entered a stall. Only after she'd locked the door behind her did she realize the other one was occupied.

"That's right," she heard the other woman say. Apparently, she was on the phone and had no problem multitasking. "Yes, I'm here now."

Ainsley tried to tune her out as she relieved herself. The lady chatted on, talking over the noise as Ainsley flushed the toilet.

She exited the stall and walked to the sink, shaking her head. She'd never understood people who talked on the phone while they were using the bathroom. Just the idea of it grossed her out.

She started to wash her hands as the woman flushed her own toilet. "Well, like I said before," she said, metal rattling as she unlocked the door. "It's time to put the big plan in motion."

Ainsley glanced in the mirror as the woman walked out of the stall. *Oh my God*, she thought, freezing in place, her hands still under the stream of water.

Micheline Anderson stood behind her, her blonde hair teased to perfection, her makeup flawless, and her blue eyes narrowed as she stared at Ainsley.

"I'll call you back later," she said into her phone. She dropped it into her purse and tilted her head to the side. "Well, well, well," she said, sauntering forward. "Look what the cat dragged in."

Ainsley glanced away and turned off the faucet, then grabbed for the paper towels.

"What brings you here, Ms. Colton?" Micheline stepped close, leaning one hip against the counter.

"I'm here to see a friend," Ainsley lied, avoiding Micheline's gaze. She tossed the crumpled paper towels into the trash can and moved to leave, but Micheline leaned out and blocked her path, forcing her to stop or run into the other woman.

"Are you now?" Micheline asked softly.

Ainsley looked up and met her eyes, and the malice she saw glowing in those blue depths nearly made her take a step back. If she'd had any remaining doubts as to what this woman was capable of, they were gone now. The woman put on a good front, and a lot of people might think she was inspiring, but Ainsley knew she was looking at the real Micheline.

Or should she say, Luella?

Curiosity burned in her chest, and Ainsley wanted to ask Micheline what she knew about the email to the Colton Oil board members. After all, Harley

Watts, the man who sent the email, was a member of AAG. And according to her cousin Spencer, Harley hadn't acted on his own initiative. He was clearly a pawn in someone else's game, and Ainsley knew in her bones she was face-to-face with the puppet master.

Something flickered in Micheline's eyes—a note of challenge, perhaps? If so, Ainsley was sorely tempted to take her up on it.

But before she could ask her first question, the restroom door opened and in walked a Marriage Institute employee. "Oh! Ms. Anderson, there you are. Mrs. Woods asked me to escort you to her office for a visit before your seminar."

Just like that, Micheline's mask slipped back into place. She turned and beamed a winning smile at the young woman. "Of course, honey. I'd be happy to follow you."

She patted Ainsley's shoulder like they were old friends. "I hope to see you again real soon." Her tone was sunny, but Ainsley recognized the statement for what it was: a threat.

Micheline and the employee left, and Ainsley leaned back against the cool tile wall, her heart racing. What were they going to do now? She'd hoped that by skipping the seminar, Micheline wouldn't see her and they could finish collecting evidence at the retreat. But clearly, that wasn't going to be the case. Her cover was as good as blown—as soon as Micheline saw Alva and Brody, she'd reveal Ainsley's true identity. She and Santiago had to get out of here, before the Woodses discovered the truth.

She left the bathroom and practically jogged down the hall toward the room where they usually had their couple's counseling session. He was probably already inside with the facilitator, waiting for her to arrive. The therapist would think it was strange when she insisted he step into the hall to talk to her, but they didn't have to worry about keeping up appearances anymore. It was time to cut their losses and get out of here.

She slowed as she approached the room, frowning when she noticed the door was closed. That was strange. Usually, the door remained open until both she and Santiago arrived. She tried the handle. Locked.

"I'm afraid we had a room change," Brody said from behind her.

Ainsley whirled around, startled by his sudden appearance. He put up a hand and took a step back. "Sorry, I didn't mean to scare you," he said with a smile. "I was just coming to put a sign on the door. The lights aren't working in this room, so you and Santiago are now meeting in the Pine Room. Do you know where that is?"

She nodded. "The other side of the building, right?"

"Yes," Brody confirmed. "Just across from the main office, in fact."

Ainsley's stomach sank. Wonderful. She'd have

to walk past Alva and Brody's office to get to Santiago. Past Micheline, who was probably even now telling Alva about her discovery in the bathroom.

There was no help for it. It had to be done. Ainsley drew up her shoulders and nodded at Brody. "Thanks." At least he didn't appear to know who she really was yet.

"No problem."

Ainsley turned and walked back down the hall, feeling Brody's eyes on her the whole way. He might not be aware that she was playing a part, but she could tell he suspected her of something.

She rounded the corner and crossed the main lobby, headed in the direction of the office. But just as she passed the reception desk, she heard someone call her name.

Ainsley turned, horrified to find Alva Woods standing by the main entrance. "Grace, can you help me for a minute?" The older woman was holding a squirming puppy and trying to carry a bag of dog food.

Ainsley approached cautiously, searching Alva's face for signs of anger. But there was no hint of malice, no indication she'd spoken to Micheline yet. Maybe her secret was still safe…

"Where did you get this little one?" she asked, reaching instinctively for the puppy. She had a soft spot in her heart for dogs of all kinds, and she'd been thinking about adopting one for a while. Maybe it was time to do so?

Alva passed the dog into Ainsley's willing arms with a smile. "Brett found her nosing around one of the outbuildings about an hour ago," Alva said. "I just ran to the store to pick up some dog food, and after the retreat Brody and I will take her to the vet." She started to walk down the hall, and Ainsley followed, cuddling the small ball of brown fur.

"She's adorable," Ainsley said. The puppy wiggled in her arms, her tongue lapping frantically at Ainsley's chin.

"Yes, she is," Alva agreed. She unlocked a room and swung the door open into the dark space. "We can keep her in here for now."

Ainsley walked past Alva, intending to set the puppy on the ground. But a sudden, sharp sting in her thigh made her cry out and jerk forward.

Almost immediately, her head began to swim. Ainsley felt her limbs grow heavy, and she set the dog on the floor before she dropped her. Lurching awkwardly, she slapped a hand onto the table in an effort to keep her balance.

Alva's face floated into her field of vision, the older woman's expression one of pure hatred. "Did you think you could get away with it?" she asked, her once-friendly tone now dripping with acid. "Did you think we wouldn't find out?"

Ainsley tried to speak, but her voice wouldn't work. She dropped to her knees, unable to stand any longer. With a grunt of effort, she lifted her hand

and swiped her finger across the locket around her neck, activating the hidden camera.

Alva smiled as Ainsley sank to the floor. "That's right," she taunted, standing over her. "You're not going to get away with revealing our secrets."

Ainsley moved her lips, working to summon the strength to call for Santiago. But all that came out was a whisper.

"Don't worry," Alva said. "You won't be here long. I'm off to find Santiago now. The two of you will soon be together again."

The announcement filled Ainsley with horror. Alva's actions made it clear she and Brody had no boundaries when it came to protecting their scam. If they got their hands on Santiago, the couple could kill them both. Given the blind loyalty of their employees, they'd have no trouble covering up the crime.

Ainsley tried to reach out, tried to stop Alva from walking away. But her fingers curled around air. Alva laughed as she stepped out of the room, and the sound echoed in Ainsley's ears as her vision faded to black.

Chapter 13

Where was she?

Santiago paced down the hall, heading for the room where they normally met for their couple's session. The lights hadn't been working, so Brody had poked his head in and told them to move to another location. He'd said he'd post a note for Ainsley, but as the minutes ticked by and Ainsley didn't arrive, Santiago had grown worried. He'd told the counselor he was going to go find her, then stepped out to do just that.

He arrived at the regular room to find the door shut and a note posted, directing Ainsley to the new spot. So why hadn't she shown up yet?

Was she back at the cabin? They'd planned for

her to leave after the couple's session, so as not to arouse too much suspicion. But had she decided to go into hiding early? And if so, why?

He set off down the hall again, his pace slower as he considered other possibilities. Had she been attacked again? He'd figured she was safe here in the main cabin, with the other retreat attendees and the Institute's employees around. Now that he thought about it though, the employees probably weren't much use in his safety-in-numbers calculations. If they were truly as brainwashed as Ainsley suspected, they were just as likely to harm her as help her.

He glanced into the rooms he passed, looking out of habit. Ainsley wasn't the type to hide without telling him; the fact that she was gone now meant something was very wrong.

Santiago walked through the lobby and toward the Woodses' office. Maybe they'd seen Ainsley. If not, he'd check the cabin and if he still couldn't find her, he'd call the police.

He stuck his head in their office, but it was empty. "Hello?" he called out. Where was everyone?

"Probably getting ready for the seminar," he muttered to himself. He stepped back into the hall, intending to leave. But just as he took a step, a low, soft sound caught his attention.

Was that a…moan?

He spun on his heel and listened hard, hoping to hear the noise again. After a few seconds passed with only silence, he called out again. "Hello?"

There it was—a definite sound of a woman in pain.

Santiago stepped forward, zeroing in on a room several feet down the hall. The door was cracked, the interior dark. But he swore the sound was coming from inside.

He carefully pushed open the door, his free hand swiping along the wall in search of a light switch. His fingers made contact with the plastic nub and he flipped it up, flooding the room with light.

He blinked as his eyes adjusted to the brightness. A large conference table dominated the room, leaving little space for much else. He glanced around, but nothing seemed out of place.

As Santiago turned to go, something on the floor caught his eye. He bent over to get a better look. Was that a trash can, or...

Ice water filled his veins as he realized what he'd mistaken for office furniture was actually someone's feet. But not just anyone's.

Ainsley's.

He rushed forward, dropping to his knees next to her. She was lying facedown, her body completely limp. He pulled her into his arms, and she moaned at the movement.

"Ainsley, come on, wake up for me," he said frantically. He felt her neck for a pulse, calming only slightly when he found the steady, strong rhythm. She wasn't dying—not yet, anyway.

She stirred, her eyelids fluttering. "That's it," he said encouragingly. "Time to get up."

"Santiago," she whispered. "They know."

"I don't care," he said, all thoughts of the Woodses and his mission to take them down flying out of his head. All that mattered was getting Ainsley to safety. She'd already been through so much for his sake—he couldn't let her suffer through more.

"Come on," he said, pulling her into a sitting position. "We're going to get you up."

Her head lolled back against his chest, but she remained awake. "I can't walk. Alva injected me with something and now I can't really move my legs." There was a note of panic in her voice, and he cupped her cheek with his hand.

"It's okay, baby," he assured her. "You will. It'll come back, I promise." He didn't know what drugs she'd been given, but they appeared to be wearing off now. Hopefully it wouldn't take much longer before she could move on her own again.

Santiago got to his feet, then bent down and gathered Ainsley into his arms. "I'm going to put you in this chair," he told her. He couldn't bear the sight of her on the floor any longer.

She tried to help him as he maneuvered her into the seat. She leaned forward, using the table to support herself. "It was Alva," she told him. "She's looking for you."

"I hope she finds me," he said darkly. He retrieved his cell phone and quickly dialed 911. Then, against the dispatcher's instructions, he hung up and called Spencer Colton's cell.

"Come quickly," he said. "Ainsley's in trouble." He rattled off the address of The Marriage Institute and hung up the phone. He didn't have time for Spencer's questions right now; he had to get Ainsley out of here before someone found them.

Santiago leaned down and slung her arm across his shoulders. "Come on, Ainsley. We need to move." The keys to the car were in his pocket; all he had to do was get her inside and they could take off and wait for the police at the turnoff to the main road.

Ainsley grunted with effort as she tried to stand. Just as he got her to her feet, she clutched his shirt with her free hand. "Santiago," she said.

He heard the note of fear in her voice and turned to follow her gaze.

Alva stepped into the room wearing a smile, Brody on her heels. The older man sized up the situation and lifted his arm, pointing a small pistol at Santiago's chest.

"Now, where do you think you're going?" he asked.

When Ainsley saw the gun in Brody's hand, she wanted to scream. Fortunately, her throat was too tight to allow any sound to escape.

Brody gestured with his free hand. "You go ahead and put her back down."

Santiago did as instructed, depositing her gently

onto the seat. She didn't want him to move away, but her arms were too heavy to lift and she couldn't grab him to keep him close.

"I think there's been a misunderstanding," Santiago said. He raised his hands to show he wasn't a threat. "Why don't we just go our separate ways now? No harm, no foul, am I right?"

Brody shook his head. "I don't think so. We've come too far for that now."

"What do you mean?" Santiago asked.

Alva sneered. "We know who you are. Micheline confirmed it. She ran into this one here in the bathroom." She pointed at Ainsley with a look of undisguised contempt. "Thought you could fool us, didn't you?"

"Honestly, I don't know why it took us as long as it did to figure out you two were frauds. You're not a couple in trouble. I've seen the way you look at each other. It's clear you're in love."

Brody's words sent a shock through Ainsley and she glanced at Santiago. Was he right? Did Santiago love her?

"Our relationship is none of your business," Santiago said, his voice low and tight. "But you're right about one thing—we're stronger together than you'll ever know."

The ferocity of Santiago's response brought tears to her eyes. Was he speaking from the heart or bluffing? Either way, it sounded like he thought their relationship was on solid ground. And in some ways, perhaps it was. They might not have a romantic future together, but Ainsley knew they would always be friends at least.

"Whatever," Brody said. "Let's go."

Santiago made no move to follow the command. "No. You're going to have to shoot me here."

Brody stared at Santiago for a moment, as if judging his sincerity. Then he shrugged. "All right. Have it your way." He turned, pointing the gun at Ainsley.

The breath stalled in her chest as she stared at the black hole facing her. Her heart beat frantically against her ribs, as though trying to escape her body.

"I'm going to count to three," Brody said calmly.

He opened his mouth again, but before he could say "one," Santiago interrupted him. "Okay, okay!" he shouted. "Whatever you want. Just leave her alone."

Brody smirked. "That's what I thought."

"It's not too late to walk away." Santiago glanced from Brody to Alva. "The police are coming. I called them as soon as I found Ainsley. They'll be here in a matter of minutes. If you let us walk out of here, I'll tell them I made a mistake."

The Woodses looked at each other. "Guess we need to move fast, then," Brody said. Alva nodded.

"I'll get her," she said, taking a step toward Ainsley. "You deal with him."

"Wait, what's happening here?" Santiago asked, alarm sounding in his voice. He blocked Alva, preventing her from reaching Ainsley. "You don't have to do this."

"We're going to take a little walk," Brody said. "Back to your cabin."

"So you can shoot us there?" Santiago spoke loudly, and Ainsley realized he was trying to draw attention to them.

Brody realized it, too. "Son, you can yell all you want," he said with a chuckle. "There's nobody around to hear you. We canceled the seminar and sent the other couples off on a guided nature meditation. It's just us here now."

"Don't you think the police will realize what you've done when they arrive and find us dead?"

"You mean, when we take them to your cabin and unlock the door to find the pair of you slumped on the sofa, killed in an apparent murder-suicide?" Brody asked.

Alva tsk-tsked. "There was such animosity between them all week, wasn't there, dear? Everyone saw it. We had complaints about your loud arguments in the middle of the night, and one of our employees had to go out there after you tossed a chair through the window."

Ainsley's blood ran cold as the woman smiled evilly. "Don't you see?" she asked. "You've been leading up to this all week. The only tragedy is that we didn't see the signs in time to stop you from killing your wife and then turning the gun on yourself."

Brody aimed the pistol at Ainsley again, his

mouth set in a hard line. "Move," he ordered Santiago. "I'm not going to ask you again."

Santiago reluctantly stepped to the side. Ainsley
could practically see the wheels turning in his mind
and knew he was searching for a way out of this situation. Her own thoughts were a jumbled mess, thanks
to the drugs and her own panic.

She glanced around the room, trying to find something, anything they could use as a weapon. But all
she saw was the table in front of her and a few plastic chairs. Nothing that would offer protection from
a bullet or a means of defense. Maybe they'd have
better luck at the cabin?

But as Alva approached her, a glint of violence
in her eyes, Ainsley knew they couldn't let themselves be taken to the cabin. If they cooperated at
this point, the Woodses would slaughter them like
spring lambs. Hell, she wouldn't put it past the couple to shoot her and Santiago in the back and make
up a story later. No, she decided, her resolve growing with every heartbeat. Ainsley wasn't about to let
this woman win. She might die today, but she wasn't
going to go down without a fight.

Alva reached her side and leaned over, wrapping
her arms around Ainsley's torso. "Come on," she
said, grunting as she tried to pull Ainsley out of the
chair. "Let's go."

Ainsley got to her feet, pleased to find she was
rapidly regaining control of her limbs. She leaned on

Alva, but not too much. She didn't want her to know just how much she weighed.

Alva took a step forward, tugging Ainsley along with her. Ainsley cooperated, looking over the top of the other woman's head to meet Santiago's eyes. She lifted one brow in a subtle gesture, and was rewarded with a flicker of recognition in his green eyes. He moved to let the pair of them pass, stepping to the side.

Once she was clear of Santiago, Ainsley wrapped her arms around Alva and let her body go limp. The smaller woman staggered under the sudden, unexpected weight, and Ainsley tightened her grip on Alva's shoulders. Alva cried out in alarm as the pair of them crashed to the ground, Ainsley landing on top of her with a satisfying thud.

Brody yelped, his attention now focused on his wife. He reached out to try to help her, remembering a split second too late that Santiago was still in the room.

It was all the time Santiago needed. Ainsley watched as Santiago picked up a chair and flung it into Brody's chest. Brody lifted his arm in defense and the gun clattered to the floor. The two men hit the ground, each one vying for the weapon. In the meantime, Alva struggled underneath Ainsley, trying to free herself. The older woman kicked and punched, but Ainsley refused to yield. She managed to grab Alva's wrists, but Ainsley's hands still weren't 100 percent on board with responding to her brain's commands, so her grip kept slipping.

Suddenly, the two men stopped grappling. Ainsley heard a muffled yelp, then someone scrambled to his feet. She looked up to see Santiago with the gun in his hand and Brody tripping for the door.

Don't do it, she silently pleaded. She knew how angry he was—the emotion was written all over his face. He hated the Woodses for what they'd done to his sister, for what they'd done to her. But shooting Brody wasn't going to fix things. If Santiago pulled the trigger, she knew it would haunt him for the rest of his life.

For a brief second, she thought he was going to let his anger rule. He lifted his arm, pointing the gun at Brody's back. Then she saw the shock wash over his face as he evidently realized what he was doing. To her relief, Santiago lowered the pistol.

Brody had just made it to the doorway when Santiago grabbed him from behind. He spun the man around, drew back his arm and landed a right hook to the jaw. Brody went down like a sack of potatoes. Alva started screaming, making Ainsley wince.

Santiago helped Ainsley off Alva, giving the woman a glare that would strip the paint off a car. "Don't you even think about leaving this room," he said darkly. "After what you've done to Ainsley, I could shoot you and not lose any sleep afterward."

Alva practically snarled as she knelt by Brody.

"You won't get away with this! Just you wait—I'll make sure you both pay!"

Ainsley couldn't resist taunting the woman. "I don't think so, Alva. I have a recording of you threatening me after you drugged me. And of Brody pointing the gun at me, and you two describing your plans for our deaths."

The color drained from Alva's face. "How is that possible?" she sputtered.

Ainsley touched the chain around her neck. "Smile," she said sweetly. "You're on Candid Camera."

Santiago laughed and pressed a kiss to the side of her head. "God, you're the best."

A commotion sounded from the lobby, shouts of "Police!" echoing down the hall.

"In here," Santiago yelled.

A few seconds later, the room was full of officers and emergency personnel. Santiago told them about the gun, and someone collected it and locked it away. Ainsley breathed a sigh of relief, allowing herself to relax now that she knew they were no longer in danger. The Woodses were taken into custody, and Santiago waved over an EMT, insisting he evaluate Ainsley.

Spencer pushed his way through the crowd. "What the hell happened here?" he asked, looking from Ainsley to Santiago and then back again. "You two mind filling me in?"

Ainsley looked at her cousin and very nearly

started crying. She didn't think she'd ever been so happy to see him. She tried to speak, but the words wouldn't come.

Someone squeezed her hand, and she glanced down to find Santiago's fingers were laced with hers. She glanced up into his warm green eyes, and in that moment, she knew they were going to be okay. She didn't have to be afraid any longer. He was here, by her side, and they were safe.

Taking a deep breath, she turned back to Spencer. "It's kind of a long story…"

Chapter 14

Two weeks later

Ainsley closed her eyes and took a deep breath, counting silently to herself. *In, one, two, three. Out, one, two, three.*

The faint sounds of birdsong played from her phone. She'd ditched the ocean waves soon after coming home from the retreat; it was too similar to the background noise one of The Marriage Institute counselors had used at the beginning of the group sessions.

Things had moved quickly in the aftermath of the retreat. After explaining everything to Spencer and showing him and the other officers the footage her hidden camera had recorded, the Woodses had been arrested and charged with attempted murder. In the following days, she and Santiago had spent hours speaking to the district attorney, laying out all their evidence and sharing their stories. As a consequence, additional charges had been filed, including fraud and several other white-collar crimes. It was exactly the outcome they'd hoped for, the one they'd worked so hard to achieve.

And then Santiago had left.

It hadn't been a surprise—Ainsley had known he would return to Phoenix once everything was over. But a small, irrational part of her had hoped that maybe, just maybe, he would change his mind.

She should have known better. After all, she'd told him she wasn't expecting more than just one night. It wasn't Santiago's fault her heart had disobeyed her mind's orders to stay out of it.

To his credit, Santiago hadn't left without saying goodbye. He'd stopped by her office about a week ago to give her an update on Ace's case.

"I spoke with Ace again," he'd said, settling into the chair across from her desk. "He didn't have anything new to share with me."

"That's a bit of a relief." Ainsley herself hadn't had a chance to connect with Ace since arriving home. She'd been focused on catching up at work and finding new ways to distract herself from missing Santiago. It was good to know her brother hadn't gotten into more trouble in her absence.

"I'm speaking with the cleaning lady in an hour, and Ace is going to send me the security camera footage from his condo. Hopefully I'll be able to find something useful."

"So this is goodbye?" Her heart had started to pound, emotions swirling in her chest as she'd fought to keep her expression neutral. *Don't cry*, she'd told herself. The last thing she wanted was for Santiago to know how much she wished things could be different between them.

"For now," he'd replied easily. "I'll be in and out of Mustang Valley as I work on the case. I hope you won't mind if I stop by?"

"Of course not," she'd said. As long as he gave her advance warning, she'd be able to control her emotions when she saw him again.

His expression had changed then, a faint smile playing at the corners of his mouth. "That was a hell of a ride, wasn't it?"

She'd nodded, a strange sense of nostalgia growing as she recalled the events of the past week. She wouldn't miss the retreat or the people there. But Santiago? She'd miss their time together very much. Once again, he'd upended her life and she was going to have to figure out a new way of moving forward without him.

"I can't tell you how much your help means to me. I couldn't have done this without you, and I want you to know how much I appreciate everything you did for me."

"It was no problem," she'd lied. "I'm just glad the Woodses are behind bars and the innocent people they hurt now know the truth."

"Because of you," he'd said.

"Because of us," she'd corrected.

He'd watched her silently for a moment. Ainsley had known by the look in his eyes and the set of his mouth that there was more he'd wanted to say. She'd sat across from him, mentally urging him to speak, hoping he'd confess to a change of heart. They were perfect together—the retreat had proven the years apart hadn't broken their bond. Why couldn't he see that? Why wasn't he willing to take a chance with her? Didn't he think she was worth it?

Whatever he'd been thinking, he hadn't shared it with her. He'd gotten to his feet and she'd done the same, walking him to the door of her office. They paused to say goodbye, and then he'd dropped his head.

Ainsley's heart had jumped into her throat. Was he going to kiss her? She'd sucked in a breath, anticipating the feel of his mouth against hers.

But his lips had landed on her forehead. A chaste gesture of affection, the kind a brother might offer to his sister. Not the kiss of lovers.

She'd waited until she was certain he'd left. Then she'd returned to her chair and quietly cried.

He hadn't called since that final visit. And while she still missed him, still ached to be near him, it was for the best. If they stayed in regular contact, it would only prolong her heartbreak. Better to rip the bandage off now and start healing than to draw out the inevitable.

So Ainsley had returned to her work and the family drama, trying to sort through all the issues surrounding the mystery of who had shot her father and where her biological brother actually was. At least Payne's condition was stable. She didn't think she could handle any more stress at this point.

Which was why she'd taken up meditation again. It wasn't a foolproof strategy, but it was better than nothing.

In, one, two, three. Out, one, two, three.

"Ms. Colton?"

Ainsley opened her eyes and pressed the button on the intercom sitting on her desk. "Yes?"

"They're ready for you."

"Thank you."

After a final set of counts, Ainsley closed the meditation app on her phone and got to her feet. She smoothed a hand down her blouse, then picked up a file folder and headed for the door.

The conference room was adjacent to her office, a small space that was furnished more like a living room than a meeting location. Two sofas bracketed a low coffee table, and a set of chairs at the far end of the space provided additional seating. There was a narrow table along the wall closest to the door, a variety of bottled waters, teas and sodas arranged on its surface.

Ainsley walked in and smiled at the scene. Most of her siblings were there; she'd called a family meeting of sorts, wanting to give everyone an update on the investigation into Payne's shooting and Ace's history.

Marlowe noticed her first and jumped to her feet. "Ainsley! Oh my goodness—how are you? I heard about the marriage retreat. What on earth were you doing there?"

Ainsley hugged her half sister, who, despite having a newborn at home, looked as beautiful as ever. "It's a long story," she said. "I'll fill you in later when we have time."

Rafe came over to greet her next, concern shining in his blue eyes. Even though he'd been adopted by Payne as a child, as far as Ainsley was concerned he was her brother in all the ways that counted. "Kerry told me some of the details," he said softly, referring to his fiancée, who was also one of the detectives working Payne's case. "Are you sure you're okay?"

Ainsley nodded, touched by his concern. "I'm fine," she assured him. "Really, I am."

"You'd better be," Grayson said. He stepped forward and wrapped her in a bear hug. Ainsley closed her eyes and soaked up her brother's strength. They were only a year apart, and out of all her siblings, Grayson was her favorite. Though she'd never admit it out loud, especially not in front of Ace.

Ainsley gestured for everyone to sit. Marlowe and Rafe sat on one sofa, and she and Grayson took the other. "I asked you all here today so we could talk about the case. I learned a few things while at the retreat, and I wanted to fill you in."

Over the next several minutes, Ainsley told her siblings about the connection between AAG and The Marriage Institute, and her run-in with Micheline Anderson. The three of them listened intently as she spoke, clearly interested in what she had to say.

The room was silent for a moment after she finished, each of her siblings processing this new information. Finally, Grayson spoke.

"What do you think she meant by 'putting the big plan into motion?'"

Ainsley shook her head. "I have no idea. But it's been bothering me ever since. She's clearly planning something. The question is, what? Does it involve us?"

"I'm sure it does," Marlowe said. "Even though Harley Watts hasn't admitted it, we all know Micheline is the one who told him to send that email to the board."

"I'm more convinced than ever that she's really Luella Smith," Ainsley said. Her siblings all nodded in agreement.

"I think that's the most likely explanation," Rafe said. "It's all too coincidental—Luella disappears into the night and a few weeks later, boom. Micheline Anderson is born."

"But where is that baby now?" Grayson asked. It

was the question they'd all been asking. "If we find him, we'll have all the answers."

"That's the problem," Rafe said. "Luella Smith's son, Jake Anderson, hasn't been seen or heard from since he left town at the age of seventeen. I'm not supposed to talk about this, but Kerry said they're having a hard time finding him."

Ainsley frowned. "Do they think he's in hiding?"

Rafe shrugged. "Hiding. Dead. Who knows?"

"Is it really that hard to find a person?" Grayson asked skeptically. "Don't the cops have that fancy software that locates people in a matter of minutes?"

Rafe fixed Grayson with a droll stare. "They do on TV. But not in real life. Besides, do you know how many Jake Andersons are out there, both in and outside Arizona? Mustang Valley PD simply doesn't have the resources to track them all down."

"Which means we'll just have to wait," Ainsley said. "Maybe we can hire a private investigator to work on behalf of the company."

Marlowe nodded. "We should definitely consider it. Anything to get this wrapped up."

"What about Micheline?" Grayson asked. "Are the police going to do anything about her?"

"Not at this time," Ainsley said. "I told Spencer what she said about the big plan and that I knew she was up to something. He agrees with me, but there isn't enough evidence to justify launching a full investigation."

Marlowe shook her head. "This lady is bad news."

"I agree," Ainsley said. "But until she actually does something illegal, we can't do anything about it."

"What about Ace?" Grayson asked. "How is he holding up?"

Ainsley shrugged. "About as well as can be expected." She filled them in on the search of his apartment and the gun that had been planted there. "Some woman named Destiny Jones said he showed her the gun and bragged about shooting Dad."

Grayson snorted. "Ace was never one for subtleties, but even that is too over the top for him."

"Tell me about it," Ainsley agreed. "But it gets better—the police tried to bring her in for more questioning, but she skipped town."

"Of course she did," Rafe said dryly. "I'm sure whoever hired her made sure she was on the first bus out of Mustang Valley after the police found the gun. Can't have her talking and undoing the frame job."

"Who do you think hired her?" Marlowe asked.

"I don't know," Ainsley admitted. "But whoever it was, I think we can assume they're connected to the one who actually shot Dad."

The group was silent for a moment, each person considering their own list of suspects.

"My money's on Selina," Grayson said. "I bet Payne told her the gravy train was running dry and she flipped out."

Ainsley tilted her head to the side in acknowledgment. "It's possible." There was no love lost between Payne's children and his ex-wife, Selina Barnes Colton. Unfortunately, Selina was an executive and served on the board of Colton Oil, so they all had to deal with her on a regular basis. Ainsley always tried to be polite, but it was difficult at times.

Marlowe looked at Rafe. "Is she a suspect?"

He shrugged. "I can't really comment."

Grayson snorted, and Rafe held up his hands in defense. "I'm not trying to be vague. I genuinely don't know. Kerry plays things close to the vest—she doesn't want the investigation overshadowed by conflict of interest claims. But I can tell you that they are exploring every angle."

A muffled commotion outside interrupted the conversation. Suddenly, the door burst open and Selina stomped inside, Candace trailing after her.

"What the hell is this?" Selina demanded.

"I'm so sorry, Ms. Colton," Ainsley's secretary said. "I tried to stop her."

"It's all right, Candace," Ainsley said. "Don't worry about it."

Selina fixed Ainsley with a glare. "What are you all doing here? I didn't get a notice about a board meeting."

"That's because we're not *having* a board meeting," Ainsley said evenly. "This is a family discussion."

Malice burned in Selina's blue eyes. "You always were such a spoiled bitch, you know that? You and your brothers." She indicated Grayson with a toss of her head. "You just couldn't stand to see your father happy."

"Sure, Selina," Grayson said sarcastically. "Whatever you say."

She sniffed. "Ace has always been out of control. I tried to warn your father about him, but he never wanted to hear it. And now look what's happened. He shot Payne. He's guilty, and you all know it."

Ainsley bared her teeth in a fierce smile. "You're the last person who should be lecturing anyone about guilt, Selina. You're the one who's been blackmailing our father for the last twenty years. Tell me, how do you sleep at night?"

"Like a baby," Selina said. She grinned, the cat who'd gotten the cream. "Believe me, sweetie, I could tell you stories that would make your hair curl. Why do you think your father keeps me around?" She laughed. "I'm not going anywhere."

"Well, we are," Marlowe announced. She got to her feet, and everyone else followed suit. "Ainsley, call me later, okay? You need to stop by the house and visit Reed. He missed his aunt."

"Will do," Ainsley promised. She followed her siblings as they all brushed past Selina and left the room. Ignoring their erstwhile stepmother, she embraced Marlowe, then Rafe and Grayson. "Love you guys."

"Love you, too, sis," Grayson said, ruffling her hair.

"Be careful," Rafe said quietly. "If you even see Micheline in town, I want you to walk the other way."

"I will," she promised. She wasn't taking any chances. If the retreat had taught her anything, it was that the people involved with AAG were unhinged. It was possible Micheline was angry that her friends, the Woodses, had been arrested. Since Ainsley had been involved in bringing them down, Micheline might target her for revenge.

"I mean it," Rafe insisted. "Do we need to get you a bodyguard?"

Santiago had wondered the same thing, but Ainsley had brushed away his concern. "I don't think that's necessary," she said, echoing what she'd told Santiago. "Micheline might be crazy, but she's not stupid. She's playing the long con here, and I don't think she's going to get distracted."

"If you say so," Rafe replied.

Ainsley watched her siblings leave. Selina walked out of the conference room and opened her mouth to speak, but before she could make a sound, Ainsley turned her back on the woman and walked into her office. She shut the door behind her with a thud and flipped the lock into place.

She heard Selina's muffled squawk of indignation, and smiled. Yes, she was being petty. But given the events of the past few weeks, Ainsley would take her pleasure where she could find it.

Santiago leaned back in his chair and sighed, surveying the stacks of paper on his desk. He'd been working on Ace Colton's case for the last few days, hardly stopping to sleep or eat. He was tired, hungry and missed Ainsley desperately.

Leaving her had been agonizing. He'd wanted so badly to return to that little cabin in the woods, shut the door and spend the rest of his life making love to her. But that simply wasn't an option. And as she'd sat across from him behind her desk, looking so professional and proper, he'd known that the magic they'd found at the retreat was gone. No matter how good things had been between them, the distance between them was back.

He never should have slept with her again.

But he was so glad he had.

The emotional dichotomy was enough to make his head spin. Things would be so much easier right now if his heart didn't ache with every breath, but at the same time, he cherished the time they'd spent together. Ainsley had given him a gift, and he would treasure it forever.

But for now, he had to make progress on this case. He owed it to Ainsley to save her brother—after everything she'd gone through for his sake, clearing Ace's name was the least he could do.

He skimmed his notes again, mentally reviewing the conversations he'd had with various people. Before leaving Mustang Valley, he'd interviewed the cleaning lady who had found Payne after the shooting. She'd been a lovely woman who had reiterated the story she'd already told the police: she'd been vacuuming in the other room, so she hadn't seen anyone leave Payne's office. Still, she'd heard the word *mom* and someone had cursed just before the gunshot. She thought it was a man's voice, but not one she recognized.

And then there was the Arizona State Sun Devils pin that had been found near Payne's prone form. According to pretty much everyone, Payne wasn't a big sports fan. Why, then, was the pin in his office? It had to be from the shooter, Santiago figured.

Mom. The pin. And Payne Colton. The three were connected, though for the life of him, Santiago couldn't see how.

As for the gun in Ace's condo? He'd reviewed the security footage and seen a figure skulking through the rooms. The camera angle didn't show their face though, so he couldn't rule out the cleaning lady. Still, he'd spoken to the police and had been told, unofficially, of course, that the body type on the surveillance from the condo matched the body type seen on Colton Oil security tapes the night of Payne's shooting.

It was far from conclusive evidence, but taken together, Santiago was convinced Ace was not the shooter. He was, however, the victim of a frame job. The fact that Destiny Jones, the tipster who had told the police about the gun in Ace's condo, had skipped town was just the cherry on top. Santiago knew once he found her, the whole house of cards would come tumbling down.

A sharp rap on his door broke into his thoughts,

and he looked up to find his sister, Gabriela, standing at the entrance to his office. "Hey, there!" He smiled for the first time since leaving Ainsley, and stood up to greet her.

She met him halfway to his desk, and he pulled her in for a hug. She squeezed him tightly, then leaned back with a frown. "Santiago," she said disapprovingly. "When was the last time you had a shower?"

"Ah…" He ran a hand through his hair, trying to remember. "The day before yesterday, I think?"

Gabriela wrinkled her nose and shook her head. "You're a mess. I came by to see if I could take you to dinner, but you're not fit for public company."

"We could order in," he suggested.

She nodded. "We'll have to."

Forty-five minutes later, they sat across from each other at the small conference table tucked into the corner of his office. She twirled spaghetti on her fork, while he lifted a piece of pizza to his lips.

"How are you?" he asked around a bite.

She grinned. "Better, now that you exposed the Woodses as the criminals they are." She pointed at him with her fork. "My attorney and I had a meeting with the judge today. She ruled that in light of the fraud committed by the Woodses, the paperwork I signed was null and void." Happiness gleamed in her eyes as she spoke. "She reinstated the original prenup, and now Eric isn't getting a dime!"

Satisfaction bloomed in Santiago's chest. This was

it—this was why he'd done what he had, why he'd talked Ainsley into helping him. Gabriela was free from her jerk of a husband, and the man who had tried to scam her was now facing some tough questions. The stress of the retreat, the danger he'd been in, it all melted away in the face of his sister's joy. Her natural sparkle was back, and he could tell she was back to her old self again.

"I'm glad to hear it," Santiago said. "I hope you're considering pressing charges against Eric?"

Gabriela nodded. "Oh, yes. My attorney says I have a solid case. Thanks to you."

He shrugged. "You don't have to thank me. Besides, I didn't act alone."

"Who helped you?" Gabriela leaned forward, obviously curious. "I've been wanting to ask you about it. I know you didn't go there alone—they wouldn't have let you stay. So who pretended to be your wife?"

"A friend of mine. Ainsley."

Gabriela's eyes widened. "Ainsley, as in your law school girlfriend, Ainsley? The woman it seemed like you were going to marry?"

Santiago shrugged, wishing his sister hadn't made the connection. "Yes."

"Wow." Gabriela leaned back, eyeing him speculatively. "I'm surprise she still talks to you, after what you did."

"What do you mean?" He sounded a little defensive, even to his own ears, but he didn't care. His own sense of curiosity wanted to know what his sister had to say.

She tilted her head to the side. "You dumped her, remember?"

"I didn't dump her, I moved for my career."

"Whatever." Gabriela waved her hand, dismissing his clarification. "The fact remains that the two of you dated for years. Dad was ready to get the family diamonds out of the safe. But then you walked away."

"It was the right thing to do," he muttered.

"Are you kidding me?"

Santiago looked up to find his sister staring at him incredulously. "What?" he asked.

"How was leaving her the right thing to do? You'd never been so happy."

"What makes you so sure that was because of her? You never met her."

"Yeah, you made sure of that, didn't you?"

Santiago looked away. "You know why I kept her away. I wasn't going to expose her to our parents."

"Because you loved her," Gabriela said, her tone making it clear he'd just proven her point.

"What does it matter now?" he asked, pushing away his plate. "That was a long time ago."

Gabriela was silent a moment, chewing a bite of her pasta. "It was. But I think you still love her."

Santiago choked on a sip of water. "Excuse me?" His sister was right, but how had she figured that out?

Gabriela nodded. "You do," she said. "And I'm willing to bet she still loves you, too."

"What makes you say that?" He heard the note of hope in his voice and hoped his sister didn't pick up on it.

She shook her head, clearly exasperated. "She helped you at the retreat, didn't she?"

"Well, yes, but only because I agreed to take her brother's case."

Gabriela leveled him with a stare. "Oh, please. Not even you are that dumb."

Santiago's face heated and he looked away. "It doesn't matter," he muttered. "We don't have a future together."

"Why not?"

He whipped his head around to look at his sister. "You know why."

She gaped at him. "Because of Mom and Dad?"

He nodded, not bothering to elaborate.

Gabriela scoffed. "You've got to be kidding me."

"I'm not." Santiago pulled a pepperoni free from its nest of cheese and popped it into his mouth. "Our family has a terrible track record when it comes to marriage. Why would I want to go down that road, when it only leads to heartache?"

He felt his sister's eyes on him and looked up to find her staring at him, her expression a mixture of shock, disbelief and confusion. "So you're telling me," she said slowly. "That you walked away from a woman who loves you, and who you love in return, because you're afraid your relationship will wind up like our parents'?"

"Well, yeah. Look at how well things worked out for you."

Gabriela shook her head. "That's because I married the wrong person! Eric wasn't right for me—I married him to get away from Mom and Dad. You and Ainsley were nothing like that."

Santiago didn't respond. He'd never before considered the possibility that Gabriela had seen Eric as a way out of the family home. He'd thought his sister had married for love, only to have it turn sour.

"Oh my God," Gabriela said softly. "You have got to be both the smartest and the stupidest person I know. How is that possible? How can you be so intelligent, and yet so clueless when it comes to relationships?"

"Hey," he said sharply. "I don't need a lecture."

"Apparently, you do," she shot back. "You found love. Do you have any idea how rare that is? But rather than hold on to it, you threw it away because you were afraid."

"Aren't you?" Santiago asked. "No one in our family has had a good relationship. No one."

"So what?" Gabriela shrugged. "You think I'm going to let other people's failures dictate how I live my life?" She shook her head. "Hell, no. Mom and Dad made our childhood miserable. I'm not about to let them steal the joy from my future, and you shouldn't, either."

Santiago didn't reply. Gabriela's words washed

over him, sinking into his mind and taking root. He hated to admit it, but she made some good points.

His mind drifted back to the retreat. Ainsley had said as much to him, hadn't she?

You're a good man, Santiago. I know you don't see it, but I do.

She'd been so understanding that night, when he'd told her about his parents and the troubles in their marriage. He'd never talked about his childhood with anyone else, never opened up like that before. Partly because he didn't like thinking about his childhood, but mostly out of fear. He'd always assumed that once people heard about his family, they'd know he was damaged.

But Ainsley hadn't thought that.

"You're not Dad." Gabriela's voice broke into his thoughts. "And even though I've never met her, Ainsley isn't Mom. You guys aren't doomed to repeat history."

"I..." Santiago trailed off, shaking his head as a new memory popped into his brain.

I could tell by the way she was looking at you that your wife still loves you.

It's clear you're in love.

Brody's words echoed in his ears. His parents had never looked at each other with love, never shown affection of any kind. What did it say about him and Ainsley that Brody Woods, of all people, thought they were in love?

"I'm going to head out," Gabriela said. She gathered up the remnants of her meal and stood. "It's clear you have some thinking to do."

Santiago nodded, feeling shell-shocked. "Thanks for stopping by."

"Of course." She kissed him on the cheek. "Thanks again for everything. You and Ainsley make a great team."

"We do, don't we?" He'd always thought so, but he liked hearing his sister say it. And now, for the first time, he began to hope there might be a way for them to stay together...

Gabriela nodded. "Not everyone gets a second chance," she said. "I'd hate to see you throw away yours."

Santiago smiled, a sense of peace filling him as he thought about Ainsley and allowed himself to dream of a future with her. Gabriela was right; he wasn't his father. She wasn't his mother. And he wasn't going to give his parents any more control over his life.

"I'm not going to," he assured her. "I'm going to make this right."

"Good," she said, moving to the door. She stopped and turned back. "Oh, and one more thing."

"What's that?"

Gabriela wrinkled her nose. "Take a shower."

Three days later

Ainsley scrolled down the computer screen, looking at the pictures and reading the short descriptions attached.

He's cute, she thought. *A little on the young side, though.*

She moved the mouse down, bringing up a new image.

Oh, now she's beautiful.

The picture showed a golden retriever, her long hair shiny and her brown eyes bright. Ainsley read the description provided by the shelter, falling more in love with every word.

Four years old. Owner surrender due to new baby. Good with pets and people.

She was perfect.

Ainsley jotted down her identification number. As soon as she got off work, she was going to the animal shelter to check out the dogs. She'd decided adopting a pet was the best cure for her loneliness in the evenings, and this pretty girl looked like she'd be a wonderful companion.

She continued to scroll through the images, but none of the other dogs captured her attention the way the golden had. Hopefully she'd still be there this evening. Maybe she should call, just to make sure…

She reached for her phone, eyes on the screen as she searched for the number to the animal shelter. A knock sounded on her door, but she didn't look up.

"Come in," she said absently.

She found the number and punched it into her phone as the door opened. She took one last look at the golden, then glanced over to see who had come into her office.

"Mustang Valley Animal Shelter." A receptionist answered the shelter phone.

Ainsley couldn't speak. Santiago stood in the doorway, holding a bouquet of flowers.

"Hello? Hello?"

Ainsley shook her head and tried to focus on the call. "Ah, yes. Hello. I'm calling about one of the dogs on your website. Is she still available?" She provided the ID number and waited while the woman checked her system.

"Yes," she said after a few seconds. "That dog is still up for adoption. Are you interested?"

"I am," Ainsley said. Her eyes never left Santiago's face. "I'm going to stop by after work."

"Wonderful," the woman replied. "You can take her for a walk if you like."

"That sounds great," Ainsley said. "Thanks." She hung up the phone and nodded at Santiago. "You're back."

"I am," he said. He walked forward and placed the flowers on her desk. "For you."

She glanced at them. "They're lovely. Thank you." What was he playing at? He'd never brought her flowers, not even when they'd been dating.

"They're from my sister," he said. "She wanted to thank you for your help with The Marriage Institute."

Ah, that explained it. Ainsley reached for the bouquet and brought it to her nose. "That's very kind of her," she said, inhaling the fragrant blooms. The potent scent was enough to make her head spin, so she placed the flowers back on her desk. She needed a clear mind to deal with Santiago.

"What brings you here?" she asked. "I'm sure you have better things to do than act as a courier for your sister."

He shrugged. "I was hoping to talk to you."

"All right." She took a deep breath. "I have time." Hopefully he'd made a break in Ace's case. She was ready for this to be over, ready to go back to her normal life.

"I owe you an apology."

Ainsley blinked. "What?" That was…not what she'd expected him to say.

"I made a mistake. Lots of mistakes, actually."

"I see," she said carefully.

He offered her a lopsided smile. "See, that's the thing. You do see me. Like no one ever has, really."

Ainsley frowned. This conversation was getting dangerously close to being personal, and she wasn't emotionally prepared for that. "Santiago—"

He held up a hand, forestalling her objection. "Please, just let me say this." He took a deep breath, then met her gaze. His green eyes shone with vulnerability, and she sucked in a breath. Never, in all the years she'd known him, had he looked so…exposed. Her heart beat hard in her chest, and a sense of anticipation slammed into her. Santiago hadn't come here to talk shop. There was something on his mind. Something big.

"Ainsley, I love you."

His declaration knocked the wind out of her, and she leaned back in her chair.

"I always have. I realize now that I always will. You're the one for me, the only one for me. I think I've known it all along, but I was too afraid to do anything about it. I walked away from you because I thought I was protecting you. Now I realize I was only trying to protect myself."

Ainsley gaped at him. She'd dreamed about this moment for years, imagining the day when Santiago would come to her and admit he'd made a mistake letting her go. Was this really happening now, or was this simply a product of her overactive imagination?

He shook his head. "You don't owe me anything. And I certainly don't deserve another chance with you. But I'm going to ask anyway. Do you think we could try again?"

"Try again?" she echoed weakly.

Santiago nodded. "I've been doing a lot of soul-searching. I realize now that I spent too many years letting my past dictate my future. I don't want to do that anymore. I want to build a life, with you. I want to marry you, if you'll have me," he said shyly.

Say yes! her heart screamed. *Do it now!*

But her brain wasn't so impulsive.

"This is quite a change of heart," she said, unable to keep the emotion from her voice. Oh, how she wanted this to be real! But Santiago had spent years feeling like marriage wasn't for him, and that they didn't have a future together. "How can I be sure you're not going to change your mind again?"

"You can't," he said simply. "Just like I can't be sure you won't change yours. But I can promise you this—if you're willing to give me another chance, I won't make the same mistakes again."

Tears welled in her eyes as emotions warred in her chest. "I want to believe you," she whispered. "I do. But…" She shook her head. "You've walked away from me twice. I don't know if I can survive a third time."

Santiago circled the desk and gathered her into his arms. She went willingly, her body desperate to be close to him even as her mind insisted on keeping him at arm's length. "Oh, Ainsley," he said. "I'm so sorry. Please believe me when I say I thought I was protecting you."

"I know that," she sniffed. "I know you still care for me. Your actions during the retreat proved it time and time again."

He ran his hand down her hair. "Tell me to go, and I will. Ask me to stay, and I will. I know I have a lot of work to do to regain your trust. But I'm going to put in the time, however long it takes."

She sniffed and leaned back. "How do you feel about couple's counseling?"

He nodded. "I think it's a good idea. Just as long as we find someone reputable."

She laughed. "That goes without saying."

"So…is that a yes?"

Ainsley smiled, feeling her world click into place. "It means, if you're willing to do the work, then so am I."

Relief stole across Santiago's face. "I am," he breathed. "We're a team. I'm just sorry it's taken me so long to realize it."

"Better late than never, I suppose," Ainsley teased.

He leaned forward and pressed his mouth to hers. His kiss was full of promise, the start of a new chapter in their story. Ainsley cupped his face in her hands and gave herself over to this man, feeling him take his place in her heart once more.

"It's always been you," he whispered against her lips.

Ainsley smiled, her tears falling freely now. Santiago leaned back and wiped them away, the pads of his thumbs caressing her cheeks. "Beautiful," he said softly.

"I don't have a ring," he said, sounding a little shy. "Unless... well, what do you think about the emerald for now?"

Ainsley smiled. "Yes. It's perfect."

He pulled the ring from his pocket and slipped it on her finger. "I'll buy you a big diamond, if that's what you want."

Ainsley shook her head, staring down at the green stone. In some ways, it felt familiar, like seeing an old friend again. "No," she said. "This is perfect." Santiago had put a lot of thought into picking this ring out, and even though she'd initially worn it as a prop, it had made her feel connected to him. It seemed fitting to use it as a symbol of their commitment now, since the marriage retreat had brought them together again.

Santiago glanced at her monitor. "Going to adopt a dog?"

Ainsley smiled. "That's the plan."

Emotion flickered in his eyes. "Any other adoptions in the works?"

She sucked in a breath. "Maybe," she said, drawing out the word. "Is that what you want?"

Santiago smiled. "I want to be with you, and for you to be happy. I told you before I don't have to be a father. But if you want to be a mother, I am one-hundred percent on board."

Ainsley's heart swelled as his words sank in. She opened her mouth to respond, but her phone buzzed on the desk, interrupting their moment. Santiago glanced at the display. "It's your brother," he said.

Ainsley bit her lip, feeling torn. "Answer it," Santiago said gently. "I'm not going anywhere."

His words warmed her from within, and she picked up her phone. "Ace? Did you get my message?"

"Yeah, I did." Ace sounded bone-tired, and she couldn't blame him. The ballistics report had come back on the gun found in Ace's condo: it was the same weapon that shot Payne.

"We need to talk about your statement," she said.

She put him on speakerphone. "I've got Santiago here with me now. Can you come to my office? We can go over the details and walk you through what's going to happen next."

"Now's not really a good time for me," Ace said.

Ainsley exchanged a look with Santiago, a kernel of worry forming in her stomach. "Ace, this is important."

"I know, Ainsley. But I'm a little busy at the moment."

"Ace," Santiago said. "The police are going to arrest you soon. You don't want them to come after you. It will look much better for you if you meet us here at Ainsley's office. Then we can all go to the police station together."

"I'm sure you're right, but that's not going to happen," Ace replied. "Look, I've got to go. Ainsley, I want you to know I appreciate everything you're doing for me. I love you."

Alarm bells started clanging in her head. "Ace, please don't do anything stupid," she pleaded. Santiago placed his hand on her shoulder and squeezed in a silent gesture of support.

"I'll try not to, but you know me. Can't be helped."

"Ace—" she said, but the line went dead before she could get another word out.

Ainsley hung up and turned to Santiago. "What is he doing?" she moaned. "This will only make things worse."

Santiago rubbed her back. "It's going to be okay,"

he said. "We'll clear his name and this will all blow over."

"I hope you're right."

The phone rang again, and this time, Spencer's name flashed across the display. Ainsley answered it, putting the call on speaker once more.

"Hello?"

Spencer didn't bother with the niceties. "Where's your brother, Ainsley?"

"I don't know. Why?"

Her cousin sighed heavily. "You know why. We need to arrest him."

"Go ahead. I'm not stopping you."

"He's not here," Spencer said wearily. "His condo is empty. No sign of him. It looks like Ace has skipped town."

Ainsley closed her eyes, silently cursing her brother and his impulsivity. "Maybe he's just running some errands?"

"Nope," Spencer said. "We've been looking for him all day. His condo hasn't been lived in for a few days at least. Ace is gone."

"Great."

"Yeah." Spencer sighed again. "Look, I know this is awkward, but if you hear from him…?" He trailed off, his question clear.

"If I hear from him in the future, I will encourage him to turn himself in," Ainsley said.

"All right." She could tell from Spencer's tone he'd been hoping for more than the standard legal response. But Ainsley wasn't about to make a promise she wasn't sure she could keep.

"Take care of yourself, Spencer," she said. It was clear he was burning the candle at both ends, trying to solve this case.

"You, too, Ainsley."

She hung up and looked at Santiago. "Well, he's gone and done it now."

"It doesn't look good," Santiago admitted. "But like I said before, I know the truth will come out in the end."

She shook her head. "Such confidence."

He grinned. "Hey, can you blame me? Now that I've got you by my side, I can take on the world. Proving your brother's innocence is just the first thing on my to-do list."

Ainsley smiled and leaned in for another kiss. "I guess we'd better get started then."

Santiago brushed a strand of hair off her cheek, his green eyes alight with love. "Together."

* * * * *

*Prosecutor Emma Martin teams up with
Officer Jayden Powell to catch an abuser and protect
a victim. But when Emma's life is put in danger, can
Jayden keep her safe—and help track down
a perpetrator?*

Read on for a sneak preview of
Shielded in the Shadows,
part of the Where Secrets are Safe series from
USA TODAY *bestselling author Tara Taylor Quinn.*

Shots rang out. At first, Jayden Powell thought a car
had backfired. Ducking behind a tree by instinct, he
identified the source as gunfire seconds before the sound
came again and he fell backward with the force to his
chest. Upper right. The only part not shielded by the
trunk he'd been using for cover.

Lying still, in agony, his head turned to the side on
the unevenly cut lawn, Jayden played dead, figuring that
was what the perp wanted: him dead. Praying that it was
enough. That the guy wouldn't shoot again, just for spite.
Or kicks.

A blade of grass stuck up his nose. Tickling. Irritating.
Damn. If he sneezed, he'd be dead. Killed again—by a
sneeze. Did his breathing show? Should he try to hold
his breath?

Why wasn't he hearing sirens?

They were in Santa Raquel, California. It was an oceanside town with full police protection—not some burg where they had to wait on County, like some of the other places he served.

His nose twitched. Had to be two blades of grass. One up inside trying to crawl back into his throat. One poking at the edge of his nostril. Maybe if his chest burned a little more, he wouldn't notice.

Where the hell was Jasper? His sometime partner and fellow probation officer, Leon Jasper, had waited in the car on this one, just as Jayden, the senior of the two, had insisted. Luke Wallace was Jayden's offender. His newest client. He preferred first meetings to be one-on-one.

Good thing, too, or Leon would be lying right next to him—and the guy had a wife with a kid on the way. A boy. No…maybe a girl. Had he actually heard yet?

Jayden was going to sneeze. If he took another breath, he'd be dead for sure. Maybe just a small inhale through the mouth. Slow and long and easy, just like he'd been doing. Right?

Shouldn't have let his mouth fall open. Now he had grass there, too. It tasted like sour bugs and…

Sirens blared in the distance. An unmistakable sound.

Thank God.

Don't miss
Shielded in the Shadows *by Tara Taylor Quinn,*
available June 2020 wherever
Harlequin Romantic Suspense
books and ebooks are sold.

Harlequin.com

Get 4 FREE REWARDS!

We'll send you 2 FREE Books plus 2 FREE Mystery Gifts.

Harlequin Romantic Suspense books are heart-racing page-turners with unexpected plot twists and irresistible chemistry that will keep you guessing to the very end.

FREE
Value Over
$20

SPECIAL EXCERPT FROM

HQN

Keep reading for a special preview of the second gripping book in the Maximum Security series from New York Times *bestselling author Kat Martin.*

Missing turns to murdered, and one woman's search for answers will take her to a place she never wanted to go.

Dallas, Texas

"I'm sorry, Ms. Gallagher. I know this is terribly difficult, but unless there's someone else who can make a positive identification—"

Kate shook her head. "No. There's no one else."

"All right, then. If you will please follow me." The medical examiner, Dr. Jerome Maxwell, a man in his fifties, had thick black hair finely threaded with gray. He started down the hall, but Kate stopped him with a hand on his arm.

"Are you…are you completely sure it's my sister?" She smoothed a hand nervously over the skirt of her navy blue suit. "The victim is definitely Christina Gallagher?"

"There was a fingerprint match to your missing sister. I'm sorry," he repeated. "We'll still need your confirmation."

Kate's stomach rolled. Her legs felt weak as she followed Dr. Maxwell down a narrow, seemingly endless hallway in the Dallas County morgue. The echo of her high heels on the stark gray linoleum floor sent nausea sweeping through her.

The doctor paused outside a half-glass door. "As I said before, this is going to be difficult. Are you sure there isn't someone you can call, someone else who could make the identification?"

Kate's throat tightened. "My father's remarried and living in New York. He hasn't seen Chrissy in years." Frank Gallagher hadn't seen either of his daughters since he and his wife had divorced.

"And your mother?" the doctor asked kindly.

"She died of a heart attack a year after Chrissy ran away." For Madeleine Gallagher, losing both her husband and her daughter had simply been too much.

The doctor straightened his square black glasses. "Are you ready?"

"I'll never be ready to see my sister's murdered body, Dr. Maxwell. But I'm all Chrissy has, so let's get it over with."

The doctor opened the door and they walked out of a hallway that seemed overly warm into a room that was icy cold. A shiver rushed over Kate's skin, and her heart beat faster. As Dr. Maxwell moved toward a roll-out table in front of a wall of cold-storage boxes, Kate could see the outline of a body beneath the stark white sheet.

Emotion tightened her chest. This was her baby sister, only sixteen the last time Kate had seen her two years ago, before she had run away.

The doctor nodded to a female assistant in a white lab coat standing next to the table, and the woman pulled back the sheet.

"Oh, my God." The bile rose in Kate's throat. She swayed, and the doctor caught her arm to steady her.

Don't miss The Deception *by Kat Martin.*
Available from HQN Books wherever books are sold.

HQNBooks.com